UP ON
CLOUD NINE

www.booksattransworld.co.uk/childrens

Other books by Anne Fine for older readers:

THE SUMMER-HOUSE LOON
THE OTHER DARKER NED
THE STONE MENAGERIE
ROUND BEHIND THE ICEHOUSE
THE GRANNY PROJECT
MADAME DOUBTFIRE
GOGGLE-EYES
THE BOOK OF THE BANSHEE
FLOUR BABIES
STEP BY WICKED STEP
THE TULIP TOUCH

Also by Anne Fine and published
by Doubleday/Corgi Yearling,
for junior readers:

CHARM SCHOOL
BAD DREAMS

www.annefine.co.uk

Anne Fine

Up on Cloud Nine

DOUBLEDAY

LONDON • NEW YORK • TORONTO • SYDNEY • AUCKLAND

TRANSWORLD PUBLISHERS
61–63 Uxbridge Road, London W5 5SA
A division of The Random House Group Ltd

RANDOM HOUSE AUSTRALIA (PTY) LTD
20 Alfred Street, Milsons Point, Sydney,
New South Wales 2061, Australia

RANDOM HOUSE NEW ZEALAND LTD
18 Poland Road, Glenfield, Auckland 10, New Zealand

RANDOM HOUSE SOUTH AFRICA (PTY) LTD
Endulini, 5a Jubilee Road, Parktown 2193, South Africa

Published in 2002 by Doubleday
a division of Transworld Publishers

A catalogue record for this book is available
from the British Library.

ISBN 0385 600712

Typeset by
Phoenix Typesetting, Ilkley, West Yorkshire

Printed in Great Britain by
Mackays of Chatham plc, Chatham, Kent

3 5 7 9 10 8 6 4 2

For my Ione,
from both sides

Stol Laid Out

★

Stol's laid out . . .

Stol's laid out on this strange bed-trolley thing. He might as well be waiting for his funeral. There's no blood in his face. No twitching or rolling. He's just a slab of dead meat on a hospital bed. I'm pretending I can't see the tube going in and the tube coming out. Or hear the pumping noises, and the occasional *shlup!*, like the sheep getting squashed by the hay bales in *Farm Freak!*

Mum hurries in. 'So where's his dad?'

'On his way. One of his junior barristers phoned to say he was just going through to the judge, to explain.'

Mum took a look at Stol, just lying there. Flat out. Not even breathing, so far as I could tell. You could see what she was thinking.

Not everyone would say it, though.

'Well, his dad's the *last* person we need.'

She'll not forget the time that Mr Oliver showed up in Casualty so furious at being called out of court, he practically started dishing out malpractice suits to all the doctors who'd spent the last two hours saving his son's life. And then he'd turned on me, as if it was my fault for suggesting we played Pirate Attack! in the first place. How was I supposed to know Stol would get so overexcited he'd start 'Yo-ho-ho'-ing, and swigging that stuff with the skull and crossbones? (Good thing I hadn't said a word about the pathetic knots he'd used to truss me up for the gangplank. If I hadn't been able to move so fast, he'd have been in the mortuary.)

'No, probably best off without Franklin.'

Mum grabbed the phone she'd left me earlier, and took off down the ward. I didn't bother following to try to listen. No-one gets straight through to Mr Oliver anyway. He's far too important. But even in emergencies Mum prefers things the way they are. If she can leave her message with Jeanine, his secretary, quickly enough, she can get off the phone before Franklin snatches it and starts all his arguing.

The nurse was bending over Stol when Mum came back.

'I told Jeanine to stop him cancelling. After all, nothing's happening.' Suddenly superstitious, she went pale and crossed her fingers. So did I, in my pocket, and together we stared at Stolly till the nurse moved off and Mum went on, 'I told her to

10

tell Franklin we'll stay here till he's out of court.'

We know what 'out of court' means. Back to chambers for discussions that might go on till midnight, or even later if the case isn't going well. But maybe this time, what with Stol having done for himself so comprehensively brilliantly, his dad will make the effort to get away sooner.

'What about—?'

What with the nurse still being well within earshot, Mum didn't finish, as she does usually, '– his daffy mum.' So I just answered, 'On a shoot. In the jungle.'

'The *jungle*?'

'Nicaragua.'

'I'm not sure Nicaragua's jungle.' But clearly even Mum had grasped this was no time for 'Start Geography'. To tell the truth, though, she did not look sorry. Esme Oliver is a menace in a sickroom. She is the sort of person who would unthinkingly lift off your sterile dressing to wipe off her nail polish. Or fetch out her hairspray in a ward of asthmatics.

'But is she on her way back?'

'No, not yet. They can't find her.'

'Can't *find* her? Is she *lost*?'

'No,' I explain. 'It's just that her assistant can't raise a signal. You see, she and the photographer have taken the models where there are no land lines in order to get that absolutely authentic sense of lost-in-the-rainforest chic to launch her new range of three-tiered mock-python and maribou waterproo—'

11

Normally Mum adores this sort of stuff. She says my bulletins from 'The World of Esme' have been one of the principal compensations for feeding Stolly pretty well every sensible meal he's ever eaten, checking his hair for nits whenever she does mine, and having him sleep over practically every other night, while trying to make sure he keeps up with his homework.

But, this time, Stol's too white, too still. She cuts me off.

'Right,' she says. 'You keep him going till I get back from seeing the doctor.'

What does she mean, 'keep him going'? But I don't argue. I just trail her to the door. 'The doctors won't talk to you,' I warn her. 'I asked a nurse and she said, if I wasn't family, she couldn't tell me anything.'

'So I'll say that I'm family.'

I panicked. 'But what if they ask you to make a decision?'

'Well,' she said, 'if they ask me which ice cream he's going to want for his supper, I'll tell them toffee pecan. And if they want a decision about how late he ought to be allowed to stay up watching telly, I'm going to be quite tough, and insist it's before ten.'

Brave stab. But Stol has sailed too close to death and I can't smile.

We both turn back to look at him. 'For pity's sake!' says Mum. 'I'll just find out what's what. And if there are any decisions to be made, I'll get back to Franklin. The man's supposed to be one of the cleverest barristers in Britain, isn't he? He can surely read a note pushed under his nose in the middle of a court case: *"Should we switch off your dear son's life support? Tick* Yes *or* No.*"'*

But simply joking about it has unnerved her worse. She has to come back to lay her hand against his cheek. 'Oh, Stolly! Stolly! What a little fool you are!'

Back at the door, she tells me sharply, 'You look after him!'

This time, I have to ask. 'What does *that* mean?'

'You know. Sit close. And concentrate. *Will* him back.'

'*Will* him?'

Now I'm unnerved as well, because it sounds so much like something from The World of Esme.

'That's right. Stay close. Don't let them send you off to the coffee shop, or anything. I'll bring you back something to eat. Just sit here and remember he's your friend. Stick with him.'

Strange. (For my mum.)

And she has slid away, round next door's curtain.

I know her. I sat very quietly, and, sure enough, I heard the nose-blow and the little sniffle. And the deep tranquillizing breaths she had to take before she could set her face, and go and ask whoever she could find what might be happening in Stol's flat silence.

On Planet Clean and Bright

I look around. It's Planet Clean and Bright that we're on now. Far cry from either of our tips at home. His bedroom is a riot. Mine's a mess. And this place hurts the eyes: the walls so white, the light so strong; even the polished floor seems to be winking.

I asked the nurse unhooking Stol's chart from the end of the bed, 'Am I allowed to have my chair this close?'

She scribbled a number inside a box. 'No need to whisper. With all the stuff we're pumping into him, this one is well away. Up on cloud nine.'

Up on cloud nine. A weird expression – and one I've heard about a million times, round about Stol. With him, the normal everyday things often stop mattering. Mum, for example, hasn't even mentioned school since she screeched to a halt outside the gates and, leaning across to push the passenger door open, explained why I'd been pulled out of class.

'Stol. In the Western General.'

'Not again!'

Stol's had more accidents than most of us have had hot dinners. Mum blames a lot of them on Esme and Franklin. ('Paint thinner? Under the *sink*?') But personally, I think it's more to do with something about Stolly.

Now that the nurse has gone, I shunt my chair along

the bed, back to the chart. I can't make head nor tail of it. It looks like something Mr Bryson would use to torture his top set in Physics. Or some quick test for Hieroglyphics 1. But, underneath, there is a clipboard with a ballpoint pen. And in my school backpack is the brand-new pad I was given for rough work.

He looks so – dead – for someone who has always been so alive, spilling with words and ideas. To look at him now, you'd find it hard to credit he's had a life. If he went now, all his past stuff would shrivel, even in our minds. The dead all vanish, unless they have some ferreting biographer to track down their life again after they've gone.

Or someone like Boswell, trailing around after them, charting it as they go. Stol helped me with my autobiography project once, way back in fourth year. Except you couldn't really call it helping, since what he did – after I'd spent about a hundred thousand hours on it – was leaf through quickly and tell me, 'You can't give in this.'

'Why not?'

'Because it's rubbish.'

'Rubbish?' I snatched it back and stared down at the carefully printed cover sheet:

My Earliest Years
by
Ian James Paramour

I flicked through. There was the photo of Gran pretending to play the piano in the great flood of

1965, with the water almost up to her knees. There was my Uncle Harry, waving from his super-duper drive-around mower. And Mum soppily pointing at a cloud like a tulip.

And, in between, written in – for me – quite unbelievably neat chunks, were the stories I'd heard all my life about Great-Uncle Caspar losing both legs in a car crash, and how Gran was arrested for taking someone's real fur coat by mistake when she left a restaurant, and how Dad's father regularly used to come home steaming, shouting that the whole family should get out of bed and pack everything, ready to move to the country and start a fresh, wholesome new life in the morning.

My project looked all right to me. 'What's *wrong* with it?'

'Well, it's supposed to be an autobiography. Stuff about you.'

'It *is* about me.'

'No, it isn't.' He took it back and flicked through again. 'It's all about your Great-Aunt Chloe and Grandfather Thing.'

'*So?* I bet yours is all about your rich Uncle Lionel, and all those aunties you hate going to visit.'

'Yes, but at least I put a heap of stuff in at the start about where I was born and how much I weighed, and all that.'

'But I don't know that stuff, do I?'

He wasn't listening. He was scrabbling through my first few pages. 'No, this won't do. You've missed out all the important bits. You'll just have to start again.'

I snatched the jotter back. 'Not likely!'

Even Stol, who can write whole novels when he's in the mood, let me off this one. 'All right. Just pull out the folder clip and shove the rest of it in at the front.'

'There isn't any "rest of it". I was just *found*. In a *cardboard carton*. Up an *alley*.'

'What was it called, this alley?'

'Robin Lane.'

He eyed me with the deepest suspicion. 'That can't be true.'

I was mystified. 'Why should I lie to anyone about that? And why would they lie to me? That's what they told me.'

'Well, it has to be nonsense. If you'd been found up somewhere called Robin Lane, the nurses would have called you Robin.'

'Not necessarily.'

'Of course they would. That is the sort of thing they do. You're forever seeing it on telly.'

And then and there, he dragged me off in front of Mum. Confronted, she went red as a radish. And it turned out I'd actually been found two alleys up.

'See?' Stolly crowed.

I stared at Mum. 'Why would you *lie*?'

She was still blushing horribly. 'It isn't *lying*,

exactly,' she tried to defend herself. 'Your father and I were hardly likely to be in a rush to explain exactly which alley it was, in case you went off to look at it.'

'What's *wrong* with my alley?' I demanded.

And it took ages to get out of her that the one I was found in was the one with the rubbish bins.

'A fitting start,' Stol often said, when we were older. And when we did Symbolism in English, I had to put up with a good deal of joshing. But at the time, he simply shrugged, satisfied his intuition was correct, then went on to nag Mum about showing him my Memory Box.

'That's up to Ian,' Mum said. 'They're his memories.'

'Not mine,' I said. 'I don't remember them.'

She wiped off that Well-you're-*supposed*-to look, and said instead, 'It's your decision. It's your box.'

But no decision's yours if you've got Stol around. So while I busied myself drawing a picture of a merry little baby sitting in a battered old carton, waving, he had a rummage through my Memory Box and, dumping the blanket in which I was found out of the way on the floor, picked out a couple of photos. 'So who's this?'

'Nurse Sarah Deloy. She was the one who first looked after me when I was brought into the hospital.'

'And this one?'

'Doris. My social worker. She brought me round here. And she made the box.'

He wasn't satisfied. He kept on at Mum till he'd tracked down a whole new starting chapter to my project. First, we waylaid the very postman who had brought the letter telling my mum and dad they were definitely getting a baby. (At the time, they didn't know it was me.) The postman had no problem remembering that morning. He said, after Mum read the letter, she shouted, 'We did it!' and chased after him and kissed him. (All Mum recalled was that he'd told her, rather sourly, that if she had taken to offering homes to other people's children, she could have his three little horrors, and welcome.)

Then Stol started positively grilling Granny. And after she gave up trying to swat him off, and had a think, things started coming back, and she remembered that, what with no-one expecting the letter that day, and Dad disapproving of alcohol because of his father, the only thing they'd had in the house to toast my future arrival was some sickly home-made rhubarb and elderberry cordial.

And even then Dad had to dig out the cork with Gran's nice silver-plated Salisbury Cathedral key-ring holder ('*Ruined* it, Ian. Completely bent the spire!') because none of them could think where to lay their hands on the corkscrew.

'Oh, *very* festive!' I said bitterly. But Mrs Tallentire was delighted with my project, and gave me a star. ('Most enlightening. I only hope Nurse

Deloy thought to bathe you very thoroughly indeed after being up that alley.') I didn't let on Stol had forced me into changing most of the first part till it was closer to the truth. And she would never have believed me anyway, since Stol was already notorious in school for being the most shocking, most dedicated liar.

Stol blames the aunts

Stol claims he's not a liar but a fantasist. He blames the aunts. Three times a year (before my family started rescuing him) he was sent off to stay with his mad aunts.

'Not *stay*,' he'd always insist. 'More, be *imprisoned*.'

The problem was that Great-Aunt Dolly, who was bossiest, was sick in the head. She had the most terrible visions, and thought the world was full of vicious strangers, all out to kidnap little kids like Stol, and keep them in cellars for ever and ever.

'Well, what about the other two?'

'They were no use. Maeve couldn't argue with a jelly, and Tilly was always busy weeping.'

'Weeping?'

'All the time. Into handkerchiefs. She was as wimpy as Maeve. So, since I wasn't even allowed in the garden in case I got kidnapped, I simply read all day.'

'All *day*?'

'Better than weeping in handkerchiefs. And some of the books were rather good. And Tilly helped with the big words.'

And maybe being imprisoned by mad aunts did something to feed Stol's imagination even more, because by the time we reached the junior school, he was well past the colourful fiblets stage and into great raging porky pies. (Sorry, *fantasies*.)

'Mythomania,' the teachers called it. They fussed and frowned. But we all loved it. It was like sitting round a telly that ran a different soap opera every day. He had so many lives. One day, he'd be an orphan, and we'd hear the terrible story of how he'd lost both of his parents in a hotel fire. Or tidal wave. Or hurricane. Next day, he would mysteriously seem to have six beautiful sisters, all born dumb, and all talented at seeing the future. The day after that, there'd be some brother who worked as a spy. Or a whaler. Or ace pilot. By the following morning, Stol would as often as not have somehow reacquired a set of parents (nothing like his own) who were meeting the queen today, or lying, mad as mops, upon their deathbeds in some foreign clime. By the end of the school week, his father would be starring in a film, but his sisters might have vanished. And the following week, he'd be back as an orphan.

'Not even your name's real,' Jack Warren dared complain once. '"Stolly"! Honestly!'

'It makes perfect sense,' he insisted. 'Stuart Terence Oliver. Stolly.'

And that was about the only bit of him that stayed the same from week to week. The teachers used to go unpicked.

'Stolly, did you tell those poor little Year Threes getting on the bus for their school trip that the world was going to end in two hours, and that's why they were being taken away?'

He'd put on his vacant-but-trapped face.

'You did, didn't you?'

'I may have mentioned that some people do in fact believe—'

'Stolly! The driver had to stop *four times*. There was *mass hysteria*! By the time the bus reached the Toy Museum, everyone was in *shreds*!'

To look at him, you'd never think he'd cause such chaos. Mum said he was cute as a button when he was little.

'Boss-eyed,' she said. 'Or so I thought. Strapped in that giant great tank of a pram of his in their front garden, picking away at his damsons.'

'Picking away at his *what*?'

(I thought it might be Mum's old-fashioned way of saying something rather unsavoury.)

'His damsons. Oh, that fancy French nanny of his certainly knew a good trick or two to keep him quiet. She'd dump him in the pram and give him an unripe damson and he'd spend hours trying to peel off its skin. Totally absorbed.'

'I thought you weren't supposed to give babies things with stones and pips and things, in case they choke.'

'He wasn't a baby, Ian. He must have been at least *four*.'

'Four? In a *pram*?'

I tackled Stol on the matter once, and all he could say was that he supposed he had found the pram comfy. And high, to see over the garden hedge. 'After all, that's how I met you.'

'No, it isn't. Mum said we met in nursery.' Stol had a tantrum and went blue, and I was fascinated. It seems I spent the next year and a half holding my breath in front of the mirror, seeing if I could go more blue than Stol had before I fell over.

'Didn't you *worry* about me?' I asked my dad once.

'What do you mean, worry about you?' he responded, outraged. 'Your mother took perfectly adequate precautions. She put down a mat.'

The Only Child Club

That was before Stol started the Only Child Club. That club kept us happy for months. We spent the best part of our time deciding the rules. As it happened, for the whole length of our joint membership, no-one else asked to join. But we still spent weeks mulling over details, in case they did. Like whether someone would be able to join us if they'd lost their brothers and sisters.

Or killed them.

'That would depend,' said Stol, 'on whether or not it was a proper accident.'

So we worked out a whole graded scale that took in how many brothers and sisters the applicant used to have, how long he or she had been alone, and whether or not they had deliberately murdered their siblings in order to be free to apply.

'Suppose it was *half* an accident?' I might suggest. 'Like taking a stupid younger brother along a cliff path in a gale-force storm.'

'What, no actual *pushing*?'

'No. Not sensibly making sure to shout, "You stay away from the edge!" every five seconds. But no actual *pushing*.'

'Tricky . . .'

We chewed these things over for hours. Sometimes we'd check with Dad when he came home. (No use talking to Mum. She used to take the line that she was too busy to listen to drivel.) Dad would peel off his overalls and look down at Stol, standing clutching the grubby sheets of paper on which we were stubbornly drafting our rule book.

'This sort of thing is a lot more up your dad's street than mine, Stol.'

But we all knew that Mr Oliver wouldn't be home for hours. And, if Stol phoned him at work, Jeanine would say it wasn't quite the moment. So Dad would welly in and have a go.

'So this hypothetical person who might – some day – *possibly* – want to join your Only Child Club didn't exactly force this poison down their brother or sister's throat, then? They just left it lying rather temptingly on the table?'

'That's right.'

'But not entirely by accident. I mean, they were really secretly hoping their brother or sister would take it?'

'That's right.'

Dad scratched his head. 'Well, I think they should be turned down.'

'Really?'

'Yes, really. I honestly believe that if you can't make a bit of an effort to act decently towards your little brother or sister, you don't deserve to be in such an exclusive club.'

'Goody!'

Later, when Stol had gone home – *if* he had gone home – Dad would say, 'You know that friend of yours is touched with the feather of madness, don't you?'

'The teachers say he's just "a little bit eccentric".'

'Teachers are paid to be polite about other people's children, Ian. You mark my words. That boy is bats.'

Then, as often as not, he'd go off muttering, 'Takes after his parents.'

Quietly. But not quite quietly enough.

Talk about quiet

Talk about quiet, this place is giving me the creeps. From time to time, I hear a rise of soft chatter from the nurses at the desk at the other end. A few of the monitoring machines from the other beds are ticking or shlupping. And I can hear Stol breathing now.

But only just.

In the end, it got on my nerves so much, I went off to the lavatory. On my way out, I found a man in overalls just like my dad's looking thoughtfully at a fire-extinguisher leaning crazily away from the wall in its bracket.

'Excuse me,' I mumbled. 'You don't happen to know anything about being in a coma, do you?'

He looked down at his janitor's overalls as if to say, Now why on earth, in all this enormous hospital brimful of doctors and nurses, would you pick *me*?

'Please,' I begged.

'Coma?'

'Just lying there.'

'What's wrong with—?'

'Him. He fell out of a window. He broke his collar-bone, both arms in several places, six of his ribs, one leg, an ankle, and he has concussion.'

'And how long has he been – just lying there?'

'All morning.'

'All *morning*?' The baffled look cleared a bit. 'You mean they've only just got done with – so to speak – pinning him together again?'

'I suppose so.'

'Doesn't sound like a coma to me,' said the janitor. 'It sounds like someone taking his time to come round from the anaesthetic.' He turned back to the fire-extinguisher. 'And if you want my opinion, if he's broken all that lot, when he finally does wake up he'll be glad he didn't hurry.'

I cannot tell you how cheered up I was. I *knew* he was the one to ask.

Ghost in the coat closet

We grew out of the Only Child Club. Or maybe I should say the Only Child Club grew into something else.

Seances. They began because Stolly was given a Ouija board for Christmas.

'For heaven's sake!' said Mum. 'As if the boy wasn't already bad enough!'

She meant about ghosts and creepy stories. He'd always been that way. As young as four, he'd strolled into the kitchen one evening when she was making supper, slid up on a chair, dipped his hand in the cheese she'd been grating, and said conversationally, 'I was very nearly caught by a ghost in your closet.'

'Nonsense,' Mum told him, swatting his fingers away from her ingredients. 'No such thing.'

He didn't argue. But he was good on ghosts. And telling creepy stories. My favourite was the one about a blind man who bumped into a plump young lady in the middle of a blackout, and asked her the way to Tannenbaumstrasse.

'Funny name for a street.'

'This was Germany, dumbo. At the end of the war. When they'd run out of food and everything.'

'So how come she was still plump?'

'I don't know. Maybe she was really, really tubby to begin with. Anyhow, this blind man showed her some letter he had to deliver, and what with the streets being such a mess after the bombing, she said she'd do it for him. But when she looked back to check he was all right, she saw him picking his way perfectly nimbly over the heaps of rubble, and got suspicious. So, instead of delivering the letter, she took it straight to the police.'

Stol's voice took on that blood-curdling tone I so adored.

'And it was just one sentence. All it said was, *"This is the last one I'll be sending you today"*.'

'Just that?'

'Just that. The police asked the plump young lady, "Wasn't there any package to go with it?" and she said, "No, just the note," and they thought, Curious! So they went round to this address on Tannenbaumstrasse, and guess what they found.'

'What?'

'Dozens of dead people, hung up on hooks like pigs in a slaughterhouse. Some of them already half cut up and put in packages.'

'What, ready to *sell*?'

'And *eat*. Black Market, see?'

I shuddered deliciously. 'And she'd have been next!'

You can see why I liked him sleeping over. And you can see why Mum was never quite so keen. But when he came round clutching the Ouija board, she tried to put her foot down.

29

'No.'

'I thought you didn't believe in ghosts and spirits and things,' Stolly accused her.

'No more I do.'

'Well, then,' he said. 'It's just a game, isn't it? I mean, if you won't even let us play a silly *game*, you must believe there's something in it.'

'Don't try your father's lawyer tricks on me, young Stol!'

But he could always work his way round Mum. And Dad was keen.

'Brilliant! We used to do this all the time when I was young. We didn't have a proper board like this, though. All we had was a circle of scrappy bits of paper with the letters scribbled on them, and an upside-down glass on the table.' He tugged Mum down beside him. 'Don't be a spoilsport, Sue. Let's get started.'

I don't know who was pushing it. But off it went.

'Who is there?'

'N-A-P-O-L-E-O-N.'

'Bonaparte?'

'Y-E-S.'

'Who do you want to speak to?'

'A-L-L O-F Y-O-U.'

'Do you have a message for us?'

'Y-E-S.'

'Tell us.'

'Y-O-U-R.'

'Go on.'

'T-U-F-F-Y.'

'Go on.'

'B-P.'

'Are you saying "Bp"?'

'N-O.'

'Did you say "Tuffy"?'

'N-O.'

'Did you say "Your"?'

'N-O.'

'You do not have a message for us, then?'

'N-O.'

'Are you Napoleon Bonaparte?'

'N-O.'

So you can see why Mum stopped worrying. And after that, whenever she saw us bent, giggling, over the Ouija board, I don't think she gave it a thought. And we had good fun. (Far more than in that stupid, rule-bound Only Child Club.) For one thing, Stolly conjured up whole cupboardfuls of spirits to amuse us. There was a dead baby who made up endless mardy poems about having been robbed of her full life. We found a sullen washerwoman called Florrie who claimed to have washed royalty's underwear, and tied herself in knots for several hours, trying to explain 'stays' to Stol. My all-time top shade was the Abyssinian horseman Tarafou, who even sent through this noise spelt 'He-*ugh!*' that he finally explained was his regular spitting. ('Disgusting!' said my mother, and forbade us to say the word out of my bedroom.) Stol favoured the Black Fairy of the Glen, an excitable spirit who was forever picking quarrels with some poor churchwarden called Albert, who kept having to rush back to wherever spirits come from to get his chapel bells rung on time. The Black Fairy's sister was another favourite. She was called Tangerina, and once gave me an excellent idea for my homework.

Dad used to pop his head around the door. 'Just let me know if Count Vacquerie's wife drops in. I have a soft spot for her.' And, if she came, he'd bring his coffee over to our table to flirt for a while.

'So, Lizzie, did this murderous Count Vacquerie of yours have one of those great hairy beards?'

'A F-I-N-E R-E-D B-E-A-R-D.'

'And have you gone off them a bit, what with the black-hearted fellow stabbing you to death while you slept in your bed, and all?'

'N-O.'

'Would you like *me* to grow one?'

'N-O.'

'Why not?'

'S-I-R Y-O-U A-R-E M-A-R-R-I-E-D.'

'Not half,' he'd sigh. 'And if I don't get that lawn mowed before lunch, won't I soon know it?' He'd tip back the last of his coffee and off he'd go. I'd slide off in his wake to cadge a snack, and Stol would sit alone at the table, his finger resting lightly on the wobbly little wooden arm, chatting to some incoherent Visitor from Beyond whom he might later claim had been speaking Egyptian.

Once, there was almost a punch-up. It was Stol's

fault. First, he told Zool, God of Tempest, about some upstart little ocean spirit called Napley's rather unlikely claim to be 'M-O-R-E P-O-W-E-R-F-U-L T-H-A-N N-A-T-U-R-E'. Zool wasn't pleased, and showed up next time Napley was about. The argument raged. We were confused because it wasn't clear where one spirit's insult ended and the other's began. But those two seemed to know, because they kept at it hammer and tongs till Mum called us at lunch time.

'I'll say this much for that stupid Ouija board. It certainly keeps the two of you quiet.'

'*Fairly* quiet,' said Dad, who'd been trying to read the paper while the God of the West Wind had pitched in on Zool's side. 'Who was that boastful one who kept banging on about having the power to unknit the very entrails of the earth?'

'That was the Ocean of the Deep.'

'It's a pity,' said Dad, 'that we're miles from the sea here. If I'd thought he lived that tiny bit closer, I'd have asked him to pop in to sort out that tangle of wiring in my mower.'

The World of Esme

A doctor came along the ward, her shoes squishing worse than mine on the gleaming bright floor tiles. 'I understand your mother wants a little word.'

I nodded. 'She went that way.' I pointed to the swing doors at the end.

'Oh, right.'

She didn't look as if she were inclined to follow. I suppose you don't spend years and years studying textbooks to waste time trailing up and down hospital corridors, looking for patients' friends and relations.

'Tell her I'll be back this way after I've been through Tanner Ward.'

'Right-ho.'

She turned away. Then she turned back. 'You do know you can get coffee and stuff downstairs in the restaurant?'

'Thank you.'

'Tell your mum, will you?' She glanced at Stol. 'Grim as he looks, I always think, at times like these, it's worse for the mother than the patient.'

I had a sudden vision of Esme, hunched in her mulberry poncho in the forest damp and knowing nothing, peacefully watching the raindrops roll and hearing the leaves rustle. Esme is good at slipping into the mood of things. She's always the one who gets people at Hallowe'en parties to act that little bit creepier or more forbidding in their bedsheets or plastic sharpened teeth. And if she joins in with charades, then suddenly everyone's trying harder, acting funnier.

I've only watched her at one of her 'shoots' once. It was in Bermondsey. Esme was doing her new 'Sin in the City' summer nightclub look. She stood beside the photographer, watching the models strut their stuff, from time to time calling out things like, 'Midriffs *ablaze*, girls!' or 'Squint with a *teensy* bit more cool!' while Stol and I sat in our beanbags, sniggering.

Not that he generally scoffs at the things that his mum does. He's proud of Esme – claims that she single-handedly rescued metallic fabrics from the fashion wilderness. But, back in those days, each time Mrs Oliver was shortlisted for Designer of the Year, I'd overhear Mum muttering to Dad that, in her own view, Esme might do better to spend a bit more time helping her very sweet son learn to knot his own school tie. It's not that Esme didn't *realize*. It was just that she always seemed to have a reason why she couldn't take the time. If Mum said anything to her when she was on the doorstep, she'd look aghast and start on about how her personal voice could not be replaced by any hired design group, and while she was lucky enough to sit at Fashion's High Table and all her new autumn surprises were 'hot, hot, hot!' then couldn't Mum, just this once, just this week, just till she'd got her new orange and silver snakeskin look properly launched in the glossies, give her a hand looking after young Stolly?

'Esme, he's been practically living here as it is!'

'Nonsense,' said Esme, hitching her gigantic faux-chinchilla ragged-fur purse higher up on her shoulder. 'He may have slept over once or twice while I was pitching my new sleepwear range to those few leading Japanese conglomerate buyers. But usually I wouldn't dream of asking you a favour.'

'Esme, a boy of Stol's age needs to spend some time at home.'

Stol poked his head out from behind the door, where we'd been listening. 'I don't mind,' he assured the two of them. 'I like it here.' He beckoned Mum, who dropped her head to hear him whisper, 'Oh, please! If you're not careful, she'll send me off to the mad aunts!'

Mum dropped the whole business at once. (She's heard more than enough about Great-Aunt Dolly's apocalyptic visions.) She left it a week, then, when he'd stayed over three nights in a row again, tried tackling things differently. 'Esme, I do wonder if you and Franklin shouldn't be putting aside a little more time for—'

Esme threw out her arms. 'Susan! It's not as if clothes are just something that people put on in the morning! That's the *trouble* with being successful. My time isn't simply some cheetah-print polyester halter top I can conjure from *nothing*.'

Once again, Mum gave up. 'Well, Esme, if you really must get back to the design house, Stol can stay over. But you and Franklin must promise you'll come for supper tomorrow, so we can discuss this.'

(Without these two behind the door, earwigging, is what she meant.)

Esme scribbled in her daybook. '*Supper. Susan*

and Geoff's tomorrow.' She looked up hopefully. 'Who else is coming?'

'No-one!' said Mum, exasperated. 'It's to *talk*. And don't start wondering what to wear, Esme. This is just casual.'

Esme gave her a very beady look, then hurried off.

Mum turned to Stolly. 'What was that all about?'

'What?'

'That look.'

'Oh, that. Well, I just think she thought you weren't being very helpful.'

'I like that!' Mum was outraged. 'You're still here, aren't you? *And* I invited them for supper.'

'Not that,' said Stol. 'The "just casual" bit. You didn't give her much of a clue.'

'Clue to what?'

'What *sort* of casual.' He reeled them off as if his mother had been chanting them over his cradle since he was born. 'Did you mean dressy casual? Or smart casual? Snappy casual? Or active, rugged or sporty casual? Or even business casual, straight from work?'

'Oh,' Mum said, chastened. 'Oh, I see. Well, that was very bad of me.' And she went off to tear her hair in the privacy of her bedroom.

They never came, of course. Esme called to cancel at a quarter past six. 'Susan! Disaster! Poor Taran's been peeking round his camera, shrieking "More *waiflike*, if you would, dear!" at the model all

37

afternoon. But, so far, all the benighted creature is managing to give us is bury-your-babe-on-the-trail *grim*. I'm *never* going to make it.'

Mum stared down at the piles of onions and cucumbers and green peppers that Stolly and I had been slicing and chopping. 'Well, what about Franklin?'

'Franklin? No chance. He says he'll be banged up in chambers for hours yet.'

'So supper's off, then?'

'If you don't mind. I hope you haven't started cooking.'

'No, no.'

'And you can keep Stol, can't you? Since it's an emergency.'

'No problem.'

Mum put the phone down. 'Well, Stol, don't say I didn't *try* to get you raised right.'

'I don't mind,' he assured her. 'I prefer it here.'

And I shouldn't think either of us thought he was lying.

Speaking of Angels

Next time the nurse came round to check – what? That he hadn't died without my realizing? – she told me, 'Someone called Jeanine phoned with a message for your mum. It's: "*Are you sure?*"'

'"*Are you sure?*"'

'Yes, that was it. "*Are you sure?*" From Frank, she told me.'

'Franklin.'

'Not one to waste words, clearly.'

Nor his time. He's no slouch, Franklin. Sometimes, when he was ordered to drop by to pick up Stol on his way home, he'd leave his finger on the doorbell longer than was strictly polite, and when Mum went to let him in, she'd find him lolling against the doorframe as if just standing still doing nothing for these first few seconds in his day had reminded him he barely had the strength to stand upright.

'Stol ready? Can I take him?'

Stol would start gathering his gear, fussing about lost shoes, and plastic fangs or chocolate buttons. He'd fly upstairs to find his precious Captain Blood Talking Cutlass. Mr Oliver would get rattled. 'Don't take too long, Stol. I'm a bit pushed tonight. My client claims God told him to slay his family, so I'd quite like to brush up on Crown v. Harmer.'

'I talk to God quite often,' Stolly informed no-one in particular as he sat on the bottom stair, tugging on his shoes.

'Really?' Mum asked politely.

'Yes,' Stol said. 'He has quite a lot of really interesting information.'

'I wonder if he's hot on tort,' said Mr Oliver. 'I have a really rather unusual case in the offing whereby—'

'I never knew you prayed, Stol,' Dad interrupted hastily. 'Except, of course, when you are forced to, in Assembly.'

'Oh, yes,' said Stol. 'In fact, when I grow up, I would quite like to be an angel.'

'Who would have thought?' said Dad, dropping to his knees to help with the laces. (Stol took an age to get on top of tying bows.) 'As far as I recall, we've never had any theological discussions at all – except for those times, of course, when we've forced you to lend a hand with the cleaning, and you've kept grumbling that you don't think the little Lord Jesus ever had to wash up the dishes, or clean the gunk out of the sink.'

'Speaking of angels,' Mum said to Franklin, 'will you be fortunate enough to get along to this year's school Nativity?'

'Not with old Hornchurch fumbling his weary way through a cut-and-dried family axe murder. Not a chance.'

Mum looked as sympathetic as she could. But after he and Stol had gone off, hand in hand, she turned to Dad. 'Well, if the Olivers end up having to do the same as last year, our PTA will be quids in again.'

I stuck my nose in. 'Why? What did the Olivers have to do last year?'

Mum looked embarrassed. I don't think she had

40

realized I was listening. 'Well, Franklin couldn't make it, so Esme brought someone along with her to video the whole thing, so Franklin could see it later.'

'So?'

'Well,' Mum admitted, 'she was world-famous, this video-maker. Won whole strings of international awards. And you don't suppose we sold all the copies for *nothing*?'

Stol ties his laces

I said to Mum, 'You realize that's your fourth cup of coffee. You'll soon be on the ceiling.'

Mum dropped the sugar packets on the cabinet beside Stol's bed. Then she dived into the shelf beneath and pulled out his trainers. Each was still knotted with one of Stol's fearful messes, with great cuts down the side where someone in Casualty must have snipped them off his feet, rather than waste time trying to unfasten them.

Mum started picking at the claggy knots, though it was obvious the shoes were ruined.

'Message from Franklin,' I told her. '"*Are you sure?*"'

'Sure about what? His coming? His not coming?'

'Jeanine didn't say.'

Mum dropped the filthy trainer in her lap. 'It

doesn't matter either way, since I'm not sure about anything.'

'Perhaps he meant about you and me staying here all day.'

'Oh, well,' she said, cheering rapidly. 'That is about the only thing that I am sure about.' And she went back to Stol's tangle. 'Remember those endless lessons?'

Who wouldn't? Stol on the bottom stair, fretting, and Mum trying for the millionth time. 'Ready? Now take it slowly, Stol. The bunny rabbit pops out of his hole—'

Stol stuck his thumb up.

'Then he runs round the tree trunk.'

Stol made a loop.

'Then he runs round the other tree trunk and pops down the hole again.'

Stol's shoelace bow fell apart.

Mum patted his knee. 'Don't worry, sweetheart. We'll have it all sorted out before you move up to the big school, I bet you.'

'We'd really better,' Stol said gloomily. 'There's only three more weeks to go.'

Devil on his shoulder

He had something else on his mind too – the devil he believed to be living on his shoulder.

'Stol, this is nonsense!' howled my dad. 'What sort of devil?'

'A tiny one. One that can move fast.'

'And what does this – I stress – *purely* imaginary fixation of yours happen to look like in your poor deluded brain?'

'I don't know. I've never managed to turn my head fast enough to see him.'

'Because he isn't there!'

'Not necessarily. It might be because he moves so fast. Perhaps by the time I look over that shoulder, he's hopped to the other.'

Dad made the curly-wurly cuckoo sign. Mum said, 'I know what we'll do, Stol. We'll settle this by taking a quick look in the mirror.'

'You can't see devils in mirrors,' Stol informed her irritably. 'I thought everyone knew that.'

Dad made an exploding noise. Hastily Mum told him, 'Geoff, would you slip out and make sure I fastened the lock on the tool shed?'

Dad rushed from the room and Mum turned back to Stol. 'No need to be a crosspatch. You know I'm only trying to be helpful.'

Stol made a face. 'I'm sorry. I just feel so *ratty*.'

'Not sleeping properly?'

'Hardly at all.'

'You do know it's ridiculous, don't you?'

'Yes.'

'But you still can't stop thinking about it.' Mum sighed. 'Stol, *nobody* has a tiny devil on their shoulder, invisible or otherwise.'

'I know, I know! I just still think he might be there.'

Mum pulled him onto her knee. (As late as a couple of years ago, Stol was still happy to sit there, so long as she made a pretence of really pulling.) 'Stol, have you told your parents about these – these—'

'Obsessive thoughts,' Stol offered helpfully.

'Little worries,' Mum corrected.

'No.'

'Well, you must. Tell them as soon as you get back tonight.'

'I'd rather hoped I might be staying,' Stol said mournfully. 'Mum's in Colombia, doing a shoot on the mysterious allure of the fedora. Dad's working late. And Anna Maddalena was hoping to go bowling.'

Mum cracked, as usual. 'Well, when you next see your father. Promise?'

'I promise.'

Next time he came, she asked him, 'What about that devil of yours? What did your dad say?'

Stol looked quite sour. 'Well, first he put me through the third degree about exactly what I thought this devil could and couldn't do, how fast it

44

could jump, and that. And then, when I asked him what he thought, he tapped his pencil on his teeth and inspected me over his spectacles.'

'And said—?'

I can't think what Mum was expecting. After all, she knows Franklin.

'He said, "In the context of your postulates, I suppose it's quite possible."'

Tough talking, *n'est-ce pas*? But it did the trick. From that day on, there was no talk of devils. I got the feeling Mr Franklin had somehow irritated Stol out of obsession. All I know is, each time I woke in the night, worrying about more down-to-earth things like ripping the back off my Geography textbook, or splashing permanent ink down my new jeans, I'd look across and see him in the other bed, dead to the world, and snuffling very softly.

New school, new passion

Mum might have lost the bet about Stol learning to tie his shoelaces properly. But she did set him off on a brilliant new passion. In our first week at the new school, Stol started the Betting Book. First, he bet me that Mr Hepzerley's hair was dyed. Then he bet Iolanthe's brother he'd grow three inches by the end of term. Then he bet anyone who'd take him on that Mrs Clarren, our teacher, would be dead before Christmas.

Before you knew it, the whole class was at it. Stol kept the book about as neat as books can be. There were four columns. Who made the bet. With whom. One wide one, to describe the bet itself. And a space on the end, to explain what had happened.

So George bet Maria he could break his ruler simply by throwing it at the ceiling. (Lost.) Iolanthe bet Henry that the hairy thing buzzing in the window was not actually a hornet. (Won.) Stol bet Luis that the chemist on the corner had only one thumb. (Lost, though there was quite a bit of argument about how much stump made a thumb.) By half term we were on the seventh page, with Arif betting Turner his big toe was longer than Stolly's. (Lost.) Amanda bet us all that Mrs Clarren, far from being at death's door, was pregnant. (Won.) Stol bet me the shadow over the laundry basket outside my bedroom was not caused by the streetlamp. (Won – can't *believe* I took that one!) And Jim McTaggart bet he wouldn't lose as many bets as Maria before Friday. (Lost.)

'Keep on with this gambling, Stol,' Mrs Clarren warned, 'and I shall put you in charge of the Christmas school raffle.'

I think she meant it as a punishment. But Stol had a good time. He went round flogging tickets off to anyone in sight, break after break, and got into some huge conversations with people about why they were too poor to buy more than a couple.

By the last week of the term, he knew everyone. *Everyone.*

And everything about them. Which led to trouble because, when I went round to his house the night before the Christmas Fayre, I found him checking off his ticket stubs against a master list. Some of them he was simply crumpling up and tossing in the wastebin. Others, he was folding to drop in the raffle pot.

'What are you doing?'

'Fixing the raffle.'

'You can't do that!'

'Why not? I'm in charge, aren't I? She put me in charge.'

'She didn't mean for you to cheat.'

'I'm not cheating. I'm working on a perfectly good principle.'

'Whose? Burglar Bill's?'

He was quite put out. 'Not at all. Karl Marx's. Jesus Christ's. And Robin Hood's.'

'Your dad says every burglar and embezzler he's ever prosecuted has claimed all they were doing was shifting stuff from someone who didn't really need it to someone who did.'

'Does he?' Stol's voice was light years away. 'I don't remember that.'

'Yes, he does. And then he tells us how many

of them are in jail now, and laughs like a drain.'

Stol couldn't have looked more indifferent. 'Oh, really?'

I watched him toss away more stubs. 'You'll be in big trouble, Stol.'

'No-one will ever know.'

And no-one did. We sat there half the evening picking out the tickets of the folk Stol deemed unworthy. I filled the bottom of the pot with crumpled paper to hide the fact that most of the raffle stubs had vanished, and covered it with a rather fine false clingfilm bottom. Next morning, at the Fayre, Stol had the sense to invite the Turkish janitor to pull out the winning tickets, knowing full well his English wasn't good enough to explain that the inside of the pot felt peculiar.

And Christopher Tanner won the bike. Den's family won the hamper. The other prizes spread good cheer where it was needed most, and Mrs Clarren confiscated the Betting Book and never gave it back again.

Thank you so much for the lovely . . .

Stol spent so much time at our house, my mother pretty well ran his life. I would have hated it if Esme and Franklin Oliver had given me orders. But, though Stol often argued, he did it in a way that made you feel he was just family.

'Oh, no! Not thank-you letters!'

'Stol, it's New Year tomorrow. Leaving them any longer is *rude*.'

'But I *hate* writing thank-you letters.'

'Fine,' Mum said. 'Your decision. I can come back with you to your house and help you gather up all your presents and return them to everyone who sent them.'

'Not likely!'

'Or you can write and thank them, just like Ian.'

He'd sigh. 'Oh, all *right*.'

Mum put the paper in a pile between the two of us, and found us pens and stuff, and one or two not quite dried-up felt pens. We'd muck about for a bit, drawing cars racing round the margins and corpses lying at the bottom of the page. Then we'd get started. I'd write the usual: *'Thank you so much for the lovely blah-blah-blah you sent me. I especially liked it because blah-blah-blah. We had a really nice Christmas, with blah-blah-blah. I also got blah-blah-blah and bleh-bleh-bleh.'* If it was a really good present, Mum made me put in an extra chunk about what we'd been doing last term, or in the holiday, so the letter would stretch over the page. Then, at the end, I'd go: *'So thank you again for the blah-blah-blah,'* and that one would be over.

I got quite good at it. I'd churn them out at some swift rate, once I got going. Stol, though, would take for ever. He would get sidetracked straight away. Every few minutes, I'd notice his hand reach out for

49

a fresh sheet, and couldn't resist starting reading his letter upside down across the table.

So Mum said, 'And what time do you call this?' Dad must have been in tip-top fighting mood because he told her, 'Eight o'clock, Esme. Don't tell me you've lost your watch.' Mum gave him her swallowed-a-scorpion look, and told him, 'Don't you be flip with me when you come home this late.' Dad dumped his briefcase on the kitchen counter. 'For pity's sake, Esme! I'm this late every night!' and she hissed, 'Not the Saturday before Christmas! Not with the Feltherams and the Harrison-Turners in there, making icy conversation over their third drink because the halfwit who forgot they hate each other and invited them for the same night hasn't thought to get home in time.' Dad looked a bit guilty and said, 'Well, no need to get your knickers in a twist. I'm back now, aren't I?' And Mum shoved her hands on her hips and said, 'Don't think you're going to slide out of it quite that easily, Franklin Oliver. I'm not one of your—' And Dad interrupted, 'All right, all right. I'm sorry!' and tipped a load of olives into the dish he had to buy her after the rocket she gave him about eyeing the beach girls in Tarasalina. He said, 'Let's not waste time standing here spatting. Let's get this grim show on the road. Who did you say I was idiot enough to invite? Not those ghastly Harrison-Turn—?'

Then, seeing the look on Mum's face, he spun round to see Mrs Harrison-Turner in the doorway, looking flinty enough to slice steel. She said something unlikely about having a headache, and—

'Mu-um! Da-ad!' I'd call. 'Stol's telling his Aunt Eva exactly what happened at his house the Saturday before Christmas.'

Dad strolled across to take a look. 'Blimey! Hair-raising stuff!' He reached for the next page. 'Struth! Did your mother really call him that? In front of *you?*'

Mum prised the pen from Stol's hand, and scanned the pages he'd finished. 'This one's all right,' she told him after a moment, handing the top one back. 'And you can send these next two just so long as you black out what Esme called your father.' She shook her head. 'But this one won't do at all.' Her eyes widened. 'Good Lord! Who would have thought it?' She read on, still shaking her head. Then, 'As for these last three pages, you can't send them, sweetie.'

Stol was completely mystified. 'Why on earth not?'

'Because it's supposed to be a thank-you letter, not the script for a five-act tragedy. Now pick up again at the top of this page, and try to turn it back into something more normal. You know the sort of thing. *"Thank you so much for the simply lovely bleh-bleh-bleh ...""*

'It was Fireside Football,' sighed Stol. He reached out for my last effort and started copying, muttering, '*Bleh-bleh-bleh.*'

'You've written "sheriff's outfit",' I reminded him, a few moments later. 'And that's what I got. You got Fireside Football.'

'It doesn't matter,' Stol said. 'It's not a real letter any more, after all, is it? No-one will bother to read it. It's only *manners.*'

'How could you do that?'

This writing business landed him in trouble, not just at Christmas, but in summer, too. We took him with us once on holiday. We don't have anything like the money Esme and Franklin have, so we do house swaps.

'They're very sensible,' Mum explained to Stol. 'People who live by the sea love being in cities. And people who live in cities adore the beach. You tell me what anyone could possibly want on a fort-night's holiday that can't be found in someone else's house.'

'A manicure?' suggested Stolly, who'd been dragged off to some pretty smart hotels by Esme when Mum couldn't babysit. 'A full body massage? World-class hair-colouring techniques? All-day organic buffet breakfast?'

Mum looked a bit put out. 'Well, maybe so. But our family do house swaps.'

And off we went to Norfolk, for two whole weeks. I had a grand time. So did Stol. He even kept a diary. And that was what caused the trouble, because he left it under the bed by mistake at the end of the fortnight, and one of the family found it and read it.

I think these Pettifer people must be murderers. Why else are there so many dug-over patches around their garden? I expect they're for freshly-buried bodies. They can't be compost heaps because Mr Paramour says they're terrible gardeners. He says their rose beds are a fright, and their back lawn is not simply unkempt, it's also parched and infested. Sue says she thinks that's typical of their lackadaisical attitude all round. (She wasn't best pleased with the state of the kitchen.) She says the beds weren't aired, their sheets are stained and nasty, and, till she got at them, the cupboard doors were swarming with large greasy fingerprints.

Ten Things That We Hate Most About This House:

1. It's cold.

2. It's grubby.

3. Their cat goes round shedding weird little scabs, without even scratching.

4. There's not enough hot water for even one good shower, let alone two.

5. *Mrs Paramour says either they haven't got any unchipped china at all, or they've locked it away rather meanly in some cupboard.*

6. *They lied about how far the house was from the shops. By* miles.

7. *Ian's dad says you can't call three steps down, around two corners, and halfway along a landing in the middle of the night 'en suite'. Not with a bladder like his, you can't.*

8. *Ian's mum says that if their washing machine does anything over and above swill the dirt round and round, she'll be astonished. It certainly doesn't begin to rinse properly.*

9. *One of their daughters has left a pile of soiled underwear under her bed. Ian's mother says, even allowing for any last-minute rush, that is disgusting. But, then again, she says they're obviously extremely slack parents, and she'd not let any daughter of hers have such raunchy posters staring down from her bedroom wall. I told Sue my mum often brings home photo contact sheets of models looking far more pouty and undressed than that, and she said, 'Let's change the subject, shall we, Stolly?' And it isn't as if these Pettifers couldn't have lashed out on a cleaner. They obviously don't waste money on clothes. If you look at*

the photo of Little Miss Stuff-Your-Knickers-Out-of-Sight way back in her pushchair, her dad's wearing this green and yellow striped woolly. And when you look at the photo of her being given some certificate about eight years later, her dad's in the very same woolly, except even tattier.
10. Oh, and they don't have a Ouija board, and I went and forgot mine.

'How could you *do* that?' Mum wailed at Stolly, when the Pettifers' letter came. 'How could you leave your diary there and not say anything? If you had told us *half* of what was in it, we would have turned the car round and driven all the way back, rather than face this embarrassment.'

She waved the letter. I couldn't see much over Stolly's shoulder. All I could catch was '. . . *deeply hurt* . . .' and '. . . *so upset* . . .', '. . . *crying all night* . . .' and '. . . *never get over it* . . .'

'Sorry,' said Stol. But it was obvious he wasn't really. He hung his head for only a few seconds, till Mum went off, and then perked up and cheerfully went on with the story he'd been telling me about some fancy old aristocrat escorting one of his lady guests in to dinner. She'd asked him, 'And, tell me, Sir George, is this lovely ancient house of yours haunted?' Sir George had replied rather testily, 'No, of course it isn't,' at which point his false teeth had flown halfway across the room and landed

behind the fender because a ghostly hand had
reached from the shadows and slapped him very,
very hard.

Someone I've never seen

While Mum was off prowling round Tanner Ward,
checking the doctor hadn't forgotten her, someone
I've never seen before popped her head round the
curtain I've tugged a few inches along its rail to stop
the nurse watching me scribbling.

'Is this your brother, dear?'

'Sort of,' I said.

'Stuart Terence Oliver?'

'That's right.'

She looked a bit bothered. 'He's got quite a fat file
on him.'

'Yes,' I admitted. 'He does seem to fetch up having
an awful lot of accidents.'

She stared at the lashings of plaster bandage, and
the splints. 'Done himself proud this time,' she said,
and flipped through the armful of different coloured
papers she was carrying, which I took to be hospital
records of Stol's accidental poisonings, cuts, breaks
and concussions.

Finally she looked up again. 'So where's Mum,
then?'

I didn't think it would do Stol much good to say,

'In Nicaragua.' So I just muttered, 'Oh, around. Back soon.'

'Good. Best have a little chat.' She peered at me. 'It sounds like a rather strange—' She hesitated a moment. '– *fall*. Have you the faintest idea why Stuart here might possibly have been up there on the—'

'It was an accident,' I broke in hastily. 'He doesn't pay attention. He's famous for it. Ask the school. He's had an awful lot of minor calamities. And every time people have worried about them, they've realized in the end that that's what they are. Just accidents. Definitely.'

She looked about as doubtful as you can get without calling someone a liar to their face. 'Well, we'll see . . .'

'Yes,' I said confidently.

She stared me out. And then she turned and squeaked off down the shiny floor. I picked up a few sheets of paper drifting in her wake, and, since she'd vanished through the swing doors at the end, stacked them neatly on the swing tray of the empty bed behind me. Then I turned back to Stol. Up at the other end of the ward, a nurse turned off something I hadn't even noticed was whirring, and the silence around us was heartbreaking. Heartbreaking.

There was a time . . .

There was a time, on the fifth level of the multi-storey car park, when he got this weird look. I led him away from the edge we'd been leaning against, and once we were safe in the lift, I dared ask him, 'So what was that all about? What were you thinking?'

'Ay-*may!*-zing,' he told me. His eyes gleamed. 'Everything made *sense*.'

'What, everything?'

'*Everything*. And I suddenly understood something really important.'

I gave him a look. 'Oh, yes? That little green men from Mars would like you to scramble up on a narrow concrete ledge and then jump from a great height?'

'No, Mr Sensible. Something about Time.'

He said it as if it had a capital letter.

'Time?'

'All of a sudden, I realized that every single minute I've been on this planet since I was born has been just that.'

'What?'

'*Time.*'

'So?' I said. 'No call to go peculiar, is it?'

'But don't you see? Time isn't anything *real*. It's only time. So suddenly I saw that all the time that's still to come won't be real either.'

'What, it'll just be time?'

'Right. So it doesn't matter.'

Whoah, there! I hear alarm bells . . .

He's got that mad glint in his eyes again. 'So if that's all life's ever been, and all life's going to be – just time chewed up and gone – then I can do anything I want with it, can't I?'

'Not around me,' I told him sourly.

See? Away with the fairies. I am practically his *minder*.

Mum came back

Mum came back with a giant, multi-layered sandwich. 'It's egg all through. All that they seem to have is egg.'

'I like egg.'

While I was eating, I watched her slump in the chair and push back her hair. Her hand caught in a tangle, and I realized, looking at her anxious face, that she wasn't wearing make-up. Not even any lipstick.

'This woman stopped by,' I warned Mum. 'She had a file on Stol—' I spread my fingers. '– *that* thick.'

'Oh, God,' she said, and closed her eyes.

I finished the sandwich and licked a few stray bits of cress off my fingers. 'So what's the story with the doctor, then? Did you manage to find her?'

'Not just her. I found another as well!' She spoke as if, in this particular hospital, people in white coats were as rare as four-leaved clovers. 'And both said the chances were excellent that Stol would just surface from concussion with nothing worse than his breaks and bruising, and a shockingly bad headache.'

It seemed almost too good to be true. 'Just what the janitor said!'

Mum flashed me a strange look, then said: 'They did a brain scan. Two, in fact. And nothing showed.'

'What sort of nothing?'

'How should I know? Bleeding, perhaps? Or swelling? Both of them talked about those. One kept on assuring me, "No untoward pressure."'

And Mum burst into tears. I looked at Stol, who's probably sent my mum into floods more times than I have, and thought: What *your* stupid brain needs, Stol, is a little *more* untoward pressure.

To be *used*.

He was bright enough in school. They all said he had a great future ahead of him, if he could stay alive and learn to tie his laces. It was Mr Fuller from Practical Workshop who worried most.

'Come *on*, Stol,' he'd urge, drumming his fingers on the workbench. 'We're not defusing a live six-hundred-pound bomb here. Just hold the screwdriver, and twist.'

He waited while Stol picked the screw up off the floor and muttered, 'Third time lucky.'

'Don't I hope so! Mandy and Jason over there are busy building a wind-powered salt-mill. I can't spend the whole forty minutes watching you try to finish your very first pair of plain book ends.'

Stol gritted his teeth and leaned over the work-bench, reciting one of the little chanty things my mother has taught him to try to help him remember. 'Now then, it's *"Rightie-tightie, leftie-loosie"*, isn't it? So, if I want to screw it in, I—'

It wasn't that he broke off muttering. Mr Fuller had clapped a hand over his mouth. 'No!' he said, visibly unravelling. 'No, Stol. I will not have these wretched nursery utterances echoing around my workshop. If you still need them, you must learn to say them silently, inside your head, or I won't be held account-able.'

Stol despaired. 'I'll never be a proper handyman, will I?'

'No,' Mr Fuller said. 'No. You will never successfully put up a shelf, or fix a dripping tap, or screw the head back on your daughter's dolly.' He saw Stol's forlorn look. 'But,' he said hastily, 'that's only my opinion, of course. Do please feel free to look for some more ebullient view from anyone who's never taught you.'

Stol still looked crushed, and so he added kindly: 'No-one is good at everything. I'm told you're excellent on the violin.'

'Oh, that,' said Stol. 'That's just a gift from God.'

Beside him, I gasped. I (who have *only* heard him practising for hours and hours, and sat in cars while he's been taking grade exams from I to VIII) couldn't help saying, 'A gift from God? Come off it!'

But Mr Fuller only shook his head and said gently, 'Oh, Stolly! Why must you turn my workshop into a den of lies?' Then he wandered back to Mandy and Jason and their wind-powered salt-mill.

Stol put down the screwdriver and, seeing my reproachful look, tried to distract me with a blood-curdling story about a spaniel who had started to scrape at the ground and unearthed a child's body.

'A boy or a girl?'

'Girl. Eightish. She had sweet blonde ringlets and dark green—'

'No! Don't describe her! It makes the nightmares worse. Just get on with the story.'

His eyes shone. 'Well, this spaniel dug her up, and she was still neatly dressed, and everything.'

'*Neatly?* From *underground?*'

'Well, you know. Nothing missing. Except for her silver chain with a mermaid charm dangling from it that she always used to wear. Naturally, everyone was horrified, and searched for clues. But there were none, and so the murderer was never found. And years went by—'

'How many years?'

You'd never stump him. 'Seventeen. And then one morning, two hundred miles away, a fisherman was digging for worms. His spade hit a tin box. He tugged it out, thinking it might be treasure, and inside were hundreds – hundreds! – of cheap pieces of jewellery – the sort little girls wear. You know. Bead bracelets. Home-strung necklaces. Plastic rings. And, in this box, right at the bottom, there was the little silver chain with the merm—'

Just as Mr Fuller had earlier, I clapped my hand over his mouth. 'Don't tell me! I don't want to know!' I took my hand away. 'It's not true, is it? Say it's not!'

He put on his wise-old-owl look, but didn't torment me by swearing it was gospel. And I must have spoken a whole lot louder than I thought, because a moment or two later Mr Fuller was back at our workbench.

'Am I going to have to separate you two?'

63

'No, sir,' said Stolly. 'I was just telling Ian here how to tie a proper hangman's knot.'

The whole *world*'s seen Stolly trip over his laces. Mr Fuller reached under the workbench and pulled out a length of cord.

'Go on, then. Show me.'

It was embarrassing. Stol stuck up his thumb, and waved a few loops about, muttering about bunnies scampering round trees and going down holes, and such.

Then he gave up.

'It's on one of our tea towels at home,' he confessed. 'TEN VERY USEFUL KNOTS. But I can only do it if I have the tea towel spread in front of me.'

'Fancy that!' said Mr Fuller. 'Because I can only *not* do it because I have remarkable self-control.'

He strolled away whistling, and then, mercifully, the bell rang.

Best sandwich I have ever had

When I came back from the lavatory, guess who was slumped in my chair, staring at Stolly.

Mr Oliver.

He had his briefcase with him, but, just for once, he wasn't absently fingering it as if he longed to brush everything round him away, and get back to the papers inside it. He was looking at Stolly. I didn't even think his face just happened to be pointed that way while he was thinking about Crown v. Next Villain. I truly believe that, just for this once, Mr Oliver was looking at, and thinking about, Stolly.

He heard my shoes squeak closer, and swung round. 'Oh, hi.'

'Hi,' I said, perching my bum on the rail at the end of the next (empty) bed.

'He doesn't look too perky, does he?' Mr Oliver said. And then he dropped the bombshell. 'Mind you, he did just flutter his eyes a bit.'

'Did he?'

I can't tell you how I felt. But I remembered something Mum once said about the people who work in daycare centres learning to keep quiet about when the babies they're minding say their first word, or take their first steps. They don't say anything, she told me, in case the mothers are upset they weren't around for something so important.

At the time, I'd thought, 'So *soft*!' But when I thought how I'd been sitting there all morning, waiting for Stol to show one tiny sign he might come back to us, and then along strolls Mr Oliver and all of a sudden . . .

Well, what Mum told me didn't seem so silly now.

'Are you quite sure?'

'Of course I'm sure.'

I didn't know what to say after that, so I said

nothing for a bit. And then: 'They've got egg sandwiches in the cafeteria.'

He dropped a hand beside his chair, to pat his
briefcase. 'That's quite all right,' he said. 'Jeanine
was good enough to send one of the Juniors out for
a sandwich, but I'm not at all hungry.'

I put on my really hopeful look. It didn't work.
Mum says that she's always suspected the best way
of getting a subtle message through to Franklin is
to hit him over the head with a heavy pan, and then
say whatever it was again very loudly.

I took a simpler tack. 'Well, can I have it?'

'What?'

'Your sandwich.'

He gave me a bit of a Well-as-it-happens-I-might-
have-felt-like-it-later look, then handed it over. It
was brilliant. The best sandwich I have ever
had. It was organic avocado and cream cheese, with
flecks of smoked wild salmon, on olive ciabatta
bread, studded with sesame. It practically made me
change my mind about doing Engineering. I wanted
to switch to Catering Studies for at least half an
hour after I scoffed it.

We sat in silence for a while, and then he asked
me, 'Where's your mum?'

I shrugged. I thought she might be back to grilling
doctors. Or phoning Dad. Or Nicaragua. I'd been so
busy writing, I hadn't asked. So I said only, 'Did she
tell you the good news?'

He perked up. 'Good news?'

'About Stol probably being all right. Except for

66

the bashes and breaks, of course. And a world-class headache.'

He slumped back. 'Yes, she told me that. But, Ian—' (That put me on my toes. He *never* calls me Ian. In my whole life, I don't believe he's called me Ian more than a dozen times. In fact, I've gone whole months convinced that Mr Oliver's forgotten my name.) 'Ian, have you the remotest idea what can have happened?'

'No,' I said. 'I suppose he was being stupid. I suppose he fell.'

'Fell? Out of the top-floor *window*?'

He looked as unconvinced as that suspicious lady had before.

'Well, maybe—' But I couldn't think of anything even halfway sensible, so I shut up.

Mr Oliver shot out of his chair and started pacing up and down. He might have been in court. 'Why would a boy in Stol's position do that? What was he doing up in the old nanny's room anyway? You only have to *stand* by that window to see the drop.' The blood drained from his face and he sat down.

'Well, that's the thing about Stol. He's like that, isn't he?'

'Like *what*?'

Whose word to choose? I did a silent test run. As I have said, the teachers use 'eccentric' if they're feeling positive (and, if they're not, they say 'damn nuisance'). Mrs Fraser calls him 'mercurial'. My dad says 'bats', or 'touched with the feather of madness'.

Some kids say 'weird'. Mum says he's 'his own person'.

None of them seemed quite the thing.

'Well,' I said. 'Stol is famous for doing really stupid things.'

He had the nerve to speak as if this came as news. 'Really?'

I felt obliged to defend myself. 'Yes. I mean, what about that time he made a raft for his gerbils?'

'Well, that was pretty daft, I do admit.'

'And the way he always tidies the queue at the bus stop.'

'Yes, a few of the locals have taken the time to pop by and mention they find that a shade irritating.'

'And when he swore that he would eat only enchiladas and gingersnaps, yea, unto death.'

'I never heard about that one.'

'It didn't last long.' I thought some more. 'And when he started building his own private Wailing Wall.'

Mr Oliver sprang to his feet again. 'Well,' he said brightly, 'I really do think I had better have one more quick word with the doctors.' He couldn't get out of the ward into the corridor fast enough. I parked myself on his warm patch, and wondered if he had any more lunch goodies tucked away. But it's probably illegal to root in a Queen's Counsel's briefcase in hopes of finding a chocolate chip cookie. So, since I'd clearly appointed myself Stol's official biographer, I picked up the clipboard and got back to my writing.

Dreamy Sleepwear for Sleepy Dreamers

Mum hurried in, glancing back nervously over her shoulder.

'Is someone following you?'

'I was just looking for Franklin.'

'He'll be back,' I said. 'He's left his briefcase. He went off to look for a doctor.'

'Yes. We bumped into each other in the corridor. I listened in, and they told him exactly what they just told us.'

She paused. I waited.

In the end, I prompted, '*And* . . . ?'

'Nothing.'

'What do you mean?'

'Just that. All Franklin did was stand there quietly, listening to what they said. He didn't pick holes. He didn't even demand any extra explanations. He didn't start to argue. He just stood there, listening.'

'Blimey,' I said. 'No wonder you're worried.'

He came back shortly after that. Mum glanced at his defeated face, and then at me. Then she dived for the briefcase. 'Franklin, I really think you'd better go. Suppose someone needs to talk to you before the court starts up again after lunch.'

'I don't know. He looks so—'

We all filled that one in. I thought 'so *different*' just as Mum said 'so *vulnerable*', and Franklin said 'so *young*'.

He was still looking forlornly at Stolly when he said, 'You'll hold the fort, then, Sue? Till I get back? And keep trying to get through to Esme?'

Mum made a noise that wasn't quite a yes, and, when he'd gone, I said accusingly: 'You didn't sound too sure of yourself. Which bit were you fudging?'

'Esme,' she admitted. 'Oh, I feel terrible.' She sprang to her feet and leaned over Stolly just as the nurse had, but without daring to lay her hand on his shoulder. 'I certainly hope he's as firmly on track as everyone keeps telling us, because I rather think I might have fobbed off his mother.'

'Fobbed off Esme? You mean you actually got through to her? And told her not to come home?'

'Not *exactly*. I mean, I did get through. In the end. And I did manage to explain Stol was in hospital. But, frankly, Esme sounded so panicked that instead of explaining exactly what had happened, I went on a bit too quickly to tell her the doctors were insisting he'd be fine. And at the moment she asked, "Should I come home, Sue?" the line was crackling so badly I could barely make out what she was saying. I'd just started to tell her, "No, this is no good, Esme. I can't hear

70

you properly," when the line went dead.'

'Just like that?'

The guilty look was back in force. 'Yes. Just after I said the word "No". And now I can't get through again. I keep getting some recording.'

'But she'll think it's just Stol being Stolly – sprained wrist, cracked shin or something – and you were telling her not to bother?'

Mum nodded.

'Well,' I said cheerfully, 'you'll be in awful trouble if things go wrong. She'll have to sit on Franklin to stop him serving you a writ. But, on the other hand, if she stays safely away in Nicaragua . . .'

I didn't have to finish. We were remembering the times she'd been told off in this very hospital for rearranging chairs in waiting rooms, and bothering senior nurses with suggestions about the uniforms. ('The problem is, pure white's so *draining*. Only the best complexions can handle it. Now if you were to switch to some more subtle shade of cream or pale oatmeal . . .')

And when Stol wasn't truly ill – simply off colour – she was the worst nurse in the world.

Mum's mind was clearly working in the same way. 'Remember when poor Stol had food poisoning?'

Do I remember? It was unforgettable. He was sent home from school for looking flushed and feeling queasy, and when next day I told Mum that he hadn't been in class, she dragged me round to his house carrying a new pack of felt pens and an

71

emperor penguin flannel with huge flapping yellow sponge feet.

And Stolly wasn't there. The only person in the house was his last nanny. I was quite pleased. (Thought I might get to keep the flannel.) But Mum was horrified, fearing the worst as usual. 'Where have they *gone*?'

Poor Anna Maddalena pointed to a phone number on the list pinned to the wall. Mum ran her finger to the other side. 'The Exhibition Centre?' She was baffled. 'Why, when she has you to look after him, would Esme take a child who's sick to the Exhibition Centre?'

'Mrs Oliver say he "pairfect".'

'Perfect?'

Five minutes later, we were on a bus. The banners strung across the building's wide steps proclaimed: NEW DESIGNS FOR A NEW AGE. Mum rather grudgingly paid for both of us, then dragged me past the displays. Some were just trestle tables piled with strangely shaped cups and kettles and lemon-squeezers, or snazzy fabrics draped on rows of rails. Others were big square spaces done up as glossy space-age kitchens or living rooms with bold wallpaper, with weird painted cityscapes on their pretend windows.

We found Stol in a mock-up of a nursery, under a sign: THE WORLD OF ESME: DREAMY SLEEPWEAR FOR SLEEPY DREAMERS. A bunny frieze ran round three sides. The lights were shaped like angels peering down on him, wings softly glowing. The nursery table was shaped like a four-leaved clover, and toys were artfully tossed around.

And in the bed lay Stolly, fast asleep, covered in spots.

As soon as she noticed us, Esme leaped out from behind her pile of catalogues. 'Don't you think he's *divine*?'

'Esme!' Mum scolded. 'For heaven's sake! The boy's got chickenpox!'

'Nonsense,' said Esme. 'Ottoline painted them on with her Number Six rouge stick. And doesn't he look darling! He simply makes it. Such a talking point! We've had journalists, photographers! Honestly, bouquets have practically been thumping at my feet all day. Everyone drags round these dreary nothing-going-on-in-them mock-up rooms, then suddenly they're standing in front of mine, and their eyes *light up*.'

'I'm not surprised,' said Mum. 'But what about Stolly? Is he warm enough? Are you making sure he has plenty of fluids?'

'Are you kidding?' winked Esme. 'I'm always checking on him. Each time he wakes up, we gather an enormous crowd. He's getting far better care here than I'd ever give him at home.'

Mum didn't argue with that. We stood around a while, and then Stol stirred, and sat up in the top-of-the-range bright blue Russian-style pyjamas with blouson sleeves and frilled neckline that he'd refused to wear at home, or bring to our house.

I snitched to Mum. 'She must be paying him.'

Mum turned to Esme, shocked. 'You're not, are you?'

Esme said, 'Listen, Sue. I'm just a can-do girl. If I enjoy an endless summer, it's of my own making. And we've been a roaring success.'

Stol took his chance. 'Can I go home with Sue and Ian now, please?'

Esme glanced at her watch. 'Well, most everyone must have been all the way round now. And they are closing shortly . . .'

'I can't take him back with me,' Mum said. 'He isn't well, poor lamb. And we came on the bus.'

'Bus?' Esme's eyes widened. 'My heavens, Sue. I thought I had a stripped-down aesthetic, but—'

Mum scorched her with a look and she changed tack. 'I'll find someone to fetch my car round. You can take that. Then I can take the chance to chat with Cristal about our new Teen Queen pregnancy smock range.' Taking Mum's arm, she dropped her voice and told her confidentially, 'Cristal's still all for big-eyed waifs on soiled mattresses. You know – the same old sooty palette! But I feel a brand-new trend gathering in the ether. I'm thinking High Society Rockettes. Steel-mesh skirts. Glittery ankle socks—'

'Stol,' Mum said, 'were you wearing those pyjamas when you arrived here?'

'God, no!' said Stolly.

And in the flurry of Mum telling Stol off for language, and Esme sending for the car, we all got away without very much more sniggering. Stol stuffed the stupid pyjamas so deep down the back of the car seat that they weren't found till he'd grown safely out of them. Pity. What with him lying there so wan and quiet, I could do with a splash of colour and a hint of ruffle to remind me of a past while I hope for a future.

Stolly Stirring

Lights on

One of the nurses just came round again on one of her checks. She looked at her watch. 'Right, Stuart,' she muttered. 'Time to prove to me that you're still in there somewhere.'

She bent over and said loudly and firmly: 'Stuart? Stuart? Wake up, please. Be a good boy for me. Wake up for a moment.'

Nothing.

'Stuart! Please try and wake up. Open your eyes for me. Just for a moment, then I'll let you sleep.'

Still nothing.

'Stuart!'

'Most people call him Stolly,' Mum explained.

'Oh, right.' She turned back. 'Stolly! Stolly! Can you wake up, please? Just for a moment. Come along, dear!'

It can't be easy, trying to brush somebody off when half of you is trussed up in plaster, and the rest is in splints. But Stol seemed to be making a stab at it. His eyes didn't open. If anything, he was scrunching them tighter. But he did mumble, 'Go *away*. Leave me *alone*. It *hurts*.'

A tear seeped out between his eyelids and down his cheek.

The nurse stood up again, satisfied. 'Excellent!' she said, ticking off one of her little boxes. 'Lights on up top. All systems go.'

Mum burst into tears again and rushed off to tell Franklin.

Seven out of sixteen

As Mum flew out, the sheets of paper I'd dumped on the swing tray of the next-door bed wafted to the floor. I picked them up again. The top one was headed, 'A Young Person's Depression Checklist', and since, flat out, Stol wasn't at his chirpiest, and I was still in official mode, I went through it and ticked off his life for him, in boxes.

1. *Problems with concentrating?* Yes. See Mrs Fraser's last big telling off, the maths test Mr Harper socked him round the head with, and

Stol's strange way of walking past his own front gate.

2. *Hard to make simple decisions?* Yes. Look no further than the school lunch queue. Some of us have grown beards down to our feet, waiting for Stol to decide what he's eating.

3. *Sleeping too much or too little?* Yes. Both. Whichever.

4. *Loss of interest in food? Over-eating?* No, neither. Stol does eat *strangely*. (After the enchiladas and gingersnaps, we had his sausages and hot milk craze.) But the *amounts* are sensible.

5. *Over-sensitivity?* Not half. When he imagined his imaginary girlfriend, Tabitha, had chucked him, he sobbed his socks off for hours. Mum was so irritated, she sent him home, even though it was obvious that Esme didn't want him.

6. *Drinking and smoking excessively?* No. Not unless you count that weird new fizzy stuff, Bilberry Brew, that he gets from the shop on the corner.

7. *A feeling life is pointless?* No. He does go on a bit about how he and I have obviously been given entirely the wrong life, forced as we are to eke out our precious early years beached up here in Nowhere-on-Sea. 'Oh, when will things *get going*?' he wails to Mum. But she ignores him, saying that existential angst is only justified in those who've already made their beds and helped tidy the kitchen, and

would he like her to find him a little job to distract him?

8. *Avoiding family and friends?* Well, family. I'll give him half a point.

9. *Thoughts of suicide?* Daily. 'If you were going to kill yourself,' he asks me practically every few hours, 'how would you do it?' With the result that we have an ever-lengthening list of methods. Poisons rank highly. So does driving off a cliff in his Uncle Lionel's Maserati. We once designed a sort of self-operating guillotine to cut our own heads off, and we've spent hours padding round his house and mine, deciding exactly which of the hooks and beams would take our weight best if we were hanging ourselves. (The old nanny's room features quite highly in that one, I will admit, because of its rafters. But then again, so does our garage. And his utility room. And Stol has always thought a body hanging down their stairwell would look quite stunning.) I'm only going to give him half.

10. *A negative attitude. Unable to enjoy anything?* Stol? Do me a favour!

11. *Self-harm?* Well, *look* at him.

12. *A loss of sex drive?* Fat chance for either of us, but I'll say no more.

13. *Loss of self-confidence?* Ha!

14. *Anxiety?* Yes, quite a lot. And with good reason when his homework's due, or the mad aunts invite him, or it's Practical Workshop.

15. *Feeling guilty about past mistakes?* No.

No rear-view mirror in the Wagon of Stol.

16. *Irritability?* No. (Though it shows up in some of those living around him.)

Leaving out number twelve (the loss of sex drive), Stol totalled seven. Personally, I'd have thought that was a definite fail. (*No. Sorry. Not depressed enough.*) But at the bottom of the page it said, '*More than three? See your doctor.*' I thought, Well, Stol has done that, hasn't he? and went on to score for myself. I bagged an even fatter ten, and if I hadn't been feeling fine before hearing about Stolly, I might have been worried.

I tried my mum next. She did rather well. Two. Hardly depressed at all. Dad came out with the best score, actually getting nil. (Perhaps he's brain dead.) And Grandpa got a full house, because, though I didn't even want to think about his sex drive, I gave him double marks for irritability, his negative attitude and avoiding friends and family.

Excellent witness

Franklin came rushing back to pick up his briefcase. 'Got to get back to court. Afternoon session.' It was clear from the spring in his step that the good news had reached him. But just to be certain, I did a quick spot check.

'Mum told you that he spoke?'

What I could only take to be a cross-examiner's glint sprang to his eye. 'So you were sitting here, were you? Within earshot?'

'Yes.'

'And you did hear?'

'Yes.'

'Clearly?'

'Yes.'

'Without any possibility of error?'

I wouldn't care to face the man in court, I can tell you. I suddenly felt quite nervous. 'I think so.'

'*Think* so?'

'*Know* so. Yes. Know so. Definitely.'

'Very well.' A terrifying pause. Then, 'What did you hear?'

(Note that? The barrister's touch. Not, 'What did he *say*?' like anybody normal. But, 'What did you *hear*?'

He cannot frighten me. I've seen the truss he had to wear for seven weeks when he had a hernia – even worn the thing on my head every time we played Earthlings!

'Stol's exact words were, "Go away. Leave me alone. It *hurts*."'

He beamed. I couldn't tell if he was pleased because Stol's brain was working properly, my tale meshed in with Mum's, or I had been an excellent witness.

Nobody understands Franklin.

Off he went.

84

Stol's not so secret life

Mum came back looking puzzled. 'There's this weird woman in the corridor. Told me she'd left me some leaflets.'

I slid the 'Young Person's Depression Checklist' out of sight under what I was writing. 'Oh, yes?'

'She says that Stolly might be leading a secret life.'

'What, like a spy?'

'Don't be daft. Hidden feelings.'

'Hidden? Our *Stol*?'

We had a good laugh about that. But it did set me thinking. Most of the boys I know are probably like me – spend practically all their time behind a mask. You slap it on when you leave home as if you're in some play. You only take it off when you feel safe, playing peek-a-boo with next door's baby, or on a car ride with your mum, or in the shower.

Stol isn't like that. He comes out with all the stuff the rest of us keep for dark nights. He doesn't try to act tough. If something hurts, he makes a noise about it. And if something worries him, he says it straight out, even if everyone else has their ears pinned back, listening.

Last week he said to Mrs Garabour, when she was chivvying him into line: 'You know, I don't believe I even want to go into Assembly. I've been getting quite scared of God lately. He doesn't make sense. And the world's full of horrors.'

Mrs Garabour gave him a slice of tongue pie as she pushed him into place. But nobody teased him. And that's the weird thing about Stol. Maybe it all began because he brazened out this business of not being able to tie his laces. But now he's like one of those jesters in Shakespeare who are allowed to mock the king. He's outside the rules, and allowed to come out with what the rest of us are feeling.

And just come out with it he does. Over the years, he's said a heap of things in class that made me suddenly not quite sure I wanted to be sitting next to him. I'd wait for the barracking to start, only to find that instead of getting an earful of jeers or a faceful of paper pellets, our double desk has set off some serious class discussion, and it's not just the teacher looking interested, and nodding.

You take the time Melissa claimed boys don't have proper feelings.

'Nonsense,' said Stol. 'When I was dumped by Tabitha, I was *destroyed*.'

I was about to remind him Tabitha had been imaginary, when I noticed that everyone had turned round and was listening.

'While she was with me,' he went on, 'my life felt as if it had some kind of sense to it. Before, my days had been a sort of blurry mess and she put order in them. "Let's play this tape"; "Come for a walk with

86

me"; "We'll talk tomorrow". And I felt more myself, too, as if I'd been some sort of flappy be-anything, go-anywhere bag of skin till she came along, like a tough frame, to put a bit of shape in me.'

I stared. If I'd said anything remotely like that, I'd have been hooted from the room. Stol says it, and they're sitting up and some of them are even nodding as if he's finally put into words some anguish they've been feeling.

'After she left, it was as if my only true support was whipped away. I felt saggy. With no purpose. No *direction*.'

And I was glad I hadn't splatted him when, moments later, he came out with something I myself thought needed saying.

'And when it comes to showing your real feelings, school doesn't help. It's just not *good* for people.'

Mrs Garabour sighed. 'I can't think of anyone in this classroom who wouldn't be a good deal the poorer for not bothering to come.'

'That's not true,' Stol insisted. 'School is quite definitely a two-edged sword.'

'What do you mean?'

'Well.' Stol waved an arm. 'Look at us! I can remember when most of us were back in nursery. And, apart from the odd grumpy day before we came down with chickenpox or something, we were all bright-eyed and bushy-tailed.'

I waited for the snorts of contempt, but nothing happened. Everyone was still plugged in, listening.

'And most of us thought we were really big cheeses. Then we moved up to junior school. And by the time half of us had been seriously picked on for being small, or fat, or stupid, or ugly—'

One or two of them were pitching in now, with real bitterness in their voices.

'– or poor.'

'– or wearing funny clothes.'

'– or having a weird sister in another class.'

Stol took up his point again. 'Well, by then probably half of the people in this room had to take a very deep breath and show some real courage to get through those gates every morning.'

Mrs Garabour was staring and everyone was silent.

'And look at us now!' Stol scrambled to his feet and, this time, when he waved his arm around, he took in all the class. 'Things don't get any easier. In fact, they get worse. Now we live by the Invisible Scorecard. Nobody talks about it, but it's there all right. Who's smart. Who looks good. Who is good at games. Who gets invited to things. Who's never teased or bullied. It just gets tougher and tougher, and you can't talk about it, not to anyone. In every class there are a few winners, but I bet most of the people in this room spend a lot of the time practically wishing a bomb would drop on them to save their lives from being made so very miserable in little bits for so many hours each day.'

Mrs Garabour made to interrupt him, but he interrupted her back. 'Oh, I know it's all only tiny things.

But they *add up*. And there's no way of complaining. Make a fuss and you can practically see the teachers thinking you're just being silly. And, though girls cry more, it's far worse for boys. When things get really mean, a boy can't run out of the class like a girl can. We have to sit and take it. We're not supposed to even *flinch*.'

Nobody's arguing. Not even Melissa. Not even when he said, 'Melissa says boys don't have proper feelings. I reckon most boys have to stop their real feelings showing. And I think it's so sad when what you truly are inside gets to be nothing more than an embarrassment. Something to hide.'

Mrs Garabour turned to the line of boys who sit at the back on the window side. 'So is that really how the rest of you feel?'

Stol didn't even give them the chance to answer. 'Yes. That's how they feel. Except that some of them keep the bags so firmly over their heads to protect themselves that they don't even feel like proper people any more, but just a list of things they do. School, games, wind band and homework, or whatever.'

'*You* don't,' said Mrs Garabour.

'No,' Stol said. '*I* don't.'

Someone at the back – Jack Warren, I think – said, 'Well, Stol's *different*.' But no-one sniggered. There were no catcalls or jeers. I think, at heart, we all knew he'd been speaking up for us. It was as if his rising to his feet in class to say all that was somehow a sign that all the rest of us might, some day, manage to get the awful bag of trying to fit in properly right off our heads (the way Stol had been *born*) and get a *real* life. He'd flapped his arms about as usual, explaining. (My dad says, 'Cut off Stol's arms and he'd be dumb.') But, to me, watching, I have to say it was as if he'd spread, not only arms, but huge wide glowing wings as well, and offered the whole lot of us something to hope for.

Fearless

The thing about him is that, right from the start, he was absolutely fearless. Not physically. No-one could slope off round a corner swifter than Stol if any biffing started. And he was as often to be found letting one of the girls read him poetry or paint his nails as kicking a ball round the dustbins in break-time.

But in things no-one else would dare do, he was reckless. No other boy I know would call his stuffed koala Dolores, and keep on bringing it to school long after the rest of us had relegated all our soft toys to the end of the bed. In the dark. And in private.

No-one but Stol would fuss to be one of the Ugly Sisters in the school play. Quite a few of the boys might have been secretly pleased if Mrs Enderby had chosen them; but they'd never have *begged* her.

('Or Cinderella, Mrs Enderby! I don't mind being Cinderella.')

And no-one but Stol would give the talk he gave last term in Oral English: *'Art and Myself: an account of the influences that have gone into the making of Stuart Terence Oliver'*. There was a tide of barracking as he began. But once he got into it, everyone settled down because it was interesting. He told us which of his nursery readers had given him nightmares. (That bit was illustrated with some pretty good slides knocked up by one of Esme's specialist advertisement layout consultants, and I must say, I wouldn't like to meet Pansy the Dancing Elephant's wicked uncle on a dark night. And Bulldozer Bill was positively creepy.) He quoted the first poem he'd ever voluntarily learned by heart, off a park bench where his Aunt Tilly used to sit while she was weeping:

> If you with litter will disgrace
> And spoil the beauty of this place
> May indigestion rack your chest
> And ants invade your pants and vest.

He told us how disappointed he had been to learn he wasn't the first person ever to notice that some names were written the same forwards as backwards. Apart from Dolores the koala, he'd chosen palindromic names for all his favourite toys. (I'd never realized.) Eve the tin snail. Anna the bath frog. Otto the cuddly lion. Bob the seal. Ava the clockwork beetle. Even Leon Noel, the plastic guerrilla fighter.

He told us about the very first time, in a theatre, he'd realized that you could enjoy being terrified. It was the Giant's pet spider in the pantomime of *Jack and the Beanstalk* that had furnished this revelation. The lights went down, and suddenly all there was on stage were two red eyes glowing evilly through the dark, and a hint of hairy tentacle. 'Then,' Stol said boldly, 'I was so scared I nearly had an accident. Now I seek out the dare-devil frisson of horror.' He spoke of things on television that had upset him so much he couldn't sleep. And the music that first made him weep. And the best books he'd read. And the way that he thought himself into computer games. And the stories he made up if he was out walking down streets on his own, and the songs that he sang in the privacy of his bedroom. And the things that he hated most about school, and the things that he liked best. And that he was writing a novel called *Victims of Slime*.

When he'd finished, we gave him a great spontaneous 'Standing O'. And Mrs Garabour said he had almost cheered her up about being a teacher, and, since no-one could follow that, we could leave early.

No-one else could have done that. And not just no-one else I know.

No-one. I truly believe that. No-one.

Party time

Not that he couldn't be just as outspoken about other people's lives. I remember my last birthday. It's on the seventh (because that was Nurse Sarah Deloy's lucky number). After the film and the bean-feast, when everyone had finally dribbled off home, he picked up the book that was a present from Nancy.

KNOW YOUR BIRTH HOUR?
THEN WORK OUT YOUR
TRUE HOROSCOPE!

'Excellent! Your mum won't send us off to bed too early on your birthday. We'll have time.'

'Yes,' I said acidly. 'Time. But not *the* time.'

He sat wrinkling his brows. I thought at first that he was worrying that, if we don't even know this is my exact right birthday, how could we even begin to work out my horoscope? Then I thought he might be wondering if it would be rude to suggest doing his stars instead. After all, it was my book.

But, as it happens, he was thinking about something else entirely.

'Ian, do you suppose your mother thinks about you on your real birthday?'

I knew exactly who he meant. But just to put him right on one thing, I made a point of answering:

'No. Mostly, today, she's been thinking about her computer exam tomorrow.'

'I meant your *real* mum.'

'Birth mum. I haven't thought about it.'

'It's a strange idea, isn't it?' While he was talking, he rooted down the back of the sofa for the unopened pack of party poppers we'd stuffed there earlier, out of sight. He emptied them between us. 'Just choose a day, any day, and have a birthday!' He divided the poppers into two piles and popped a streamer over me. 'How old were you when they told you?'

I popped him back. 'They never "told" me. I can't remember ever not knowing.'

'Does it feel weird?'

'What?'

'You know. Not being sure which bits of you are coming from someone else you don't even know. Like how you still suck your thumb when you're tired, or the way your lips go funny whenever you eat pineapple.'

'I do not still suck my thumb.'

He didn't argue. He was off on a fresh tack. Popping another streamer over me, he started off, 'We don't even know what happened to your mum, do we? Or your dad. I bet your dad, at least, is still out there somewhere. He probably doesn't even know that you've been born. He probably broke up with your mother even before she realized you were on the way.'

I popped him in the face. He scraped the streamer

94

off and kept going. 'You realize what might happen. You might be walking along the street some day, minding your own business, and see a person who looks exactly like you except twenty years older.' He popped another streamer over me. 'Like looking in a Mirror of Time.'

I stole one of his poppers. He scooped up his last few and tucked them behind him. 'Maybe you even have brothers and sisters out there. Have you thought of that? Real brothers and sisters you don't even know about. Maybe, after you were dumped in that cardboard carton, your real parents—'

'*Birth* parents.'

'– birth parents met again, and this time they married and had kids and were happy. Maybe they lie awake each night thinking about you.' I waited till he opened his mouth again and popped a streamer. He picked the damp flecks of coloured tissue from his mouth. 'Maybe they sob in their pillows because the one thing keeping them from perfect happiness is that they can't find you.'

I wrapped the next streamer round his ear. 'They could if they wanted.'

'Perhaps they don't know that.'

'If they were looking, I'd know. There's a register. And if you're on it and the other side wants to get in touch, people like Doris arrange it.'

'Maybe they're waiting already.'

'No, they're not.'

'Maybe Sue and Geoff are lying about it. Maybe

they love you so much, they don't want you to know that your *real* parents—'

'Birth parents.'

'Whatever – are desperate to have you back. Maybe you've been sent millions of letters, and your parents have burned every one. Maybe this family you don't even know about are living in misery, unable to sleep, waiting for the post each day, praying there'll be a letter from you or from Doris.'

'Not very likely.'

But nothing stops Stol when he's on a roll. 'Maybe before she adopted you, your mum would have liked to be an actress. Maybe this is her finest role, brilliantly keeping you off the scent of your own real parents.'

Just at that moment, Mum poked her head round the door. 'You two! Clear up this mess, please.'

'Maybe your real parents—' This time I couldn't be bothered, but he corrected himself. '– *birth* parents are really easy-going, not like Sue, always making us clear up. Maybe they even have servants who pick up after parties. And maybe, for birthdays, instead of films and stuff, they jet a group of friends off to amazing funfairs in Florida and California, or do exciting things like stock-car racing, and wind-surfing.'

Best let him run down, like a clock. I just stopped listening. Mum says one day I might want to know more. When I have my own kids, maybe; or if people keep asking, 'Is there diabetes in your family?'

Maybe. But right now, if I'm honest, I'm not bothered at all. Sometimes I even feel guilty, as if adoption might be wasted on someone like me. Sometimes I think it would have been a whole lot fairer if it had happened instead to someone like Stolly, with the imagination to use it.

Tom Dunn's exam

Sometimes this gift Stol has of seeing things, not as they are, but how they could be comes in useful. Take Tom Dunn's exam. Tom was one of the school layabouts. Last year, all he seemed to do was grow taller, get tougher, and go on about wanting to be a gunner in the army.

'Armies have uniforms,' Mr Fuller kept reminding him. 'And a good deal of what you choose to turn up in most mornings bears no resemblance whatsoever to this school's chosen garb. Perhaps it's time to consider a fresh career path.'

He'd send him home. Sometimes Tom came back dressed more like the rest of us. Sometimes he didn't bother.

Mrs Garabour would go mad. 'It's not the old days now, Tom. To get on in the army, you need qualifications. And that means passing your *exams.*'

He'd grunt and ignore her. When time got pressing, Mrs Garabour lifted the imaginary sub-machine-gun out of his hands and had one of her little chats with him. 'Scorched off my socks,' he said later. 'Gave me lunch-time and after-school detentions right till the exams, just so I'll get the work done.'

And so he did, under her steely eye. The problem came when, on the morning of his first two-hour paper, he showed up in hip-hop flappy trousers, one of his dad's old striped sweaters and a pair of grubby trainers. As he strode into the exam hall, Mr Fuller caught hold of him. 'These are school hours,' he reminded Tom. 'And candidates for public examin-ations should be in proper uniform.'

Tom probably would have got away with a deep sigh and a ticking off, or another detention. Except that, in a fit of exam nerves, he was daft enough to respond: 'Well, I don't care. You can't stop me.'

So he was thrown out.

That's how, just as the maths exam was supposed to start, Mr Kinnear found him wandering past the girls' lavatories, clutching his ruler and calculator and looking as dazed as if some other army's gunners had given him a pounding. 'Tom?' he said. 'Why, after all Mrs Garabour's hard work, are you still to be found skulking in the wrong direction along corridors of under-achievement?'

Tom looked quite blank. Stol, who was hurrying along to the exam after a bit of trouble with his laces, translated for him. 'What he means is, why aren't you going the same way as me and Ian?'

'Thrown out,' Tom grunted. 'Said I wasn't dressed right.'

Mr Kinnear looked horrified. But it was Stol who solved the problem. Quick as a flash, he stopped Madge Henry on her way into the girls' lavatories. 'Quick!' he said. 'Take off your top and skirt.'

'Go boil your head, Stol.'

'No,' he explained, already tugging Tom's striped sweater off over his head. 'He needs proper uniform to sit an exam. You're in it. Quick! Get out of it!' Already, he was ordering Tom out of his flappy trousers. 'Come on, Madge. Your country needs you. Help Tom join the army.'

'Well, so long as he promises to *go*.' She didn't quite add, '– and get killed,' but you could certainly hear her think it. Especially when she had to pull Tom's quite disgusting trousers up, before unbuttoning her skirt to step out of it.

Stol handed her Tom's sweater. 'And your top.'

She did the weirdest thing I've ever seen, but, sure enough, after a few strange bulges, out it came suddenly from under Tom's sweater.

Tom climbed into the skirt.

'Shoes!' Stol said, looking down at mine, which were too small by far. Stol's feet are even smaller. In the end, with a great martyred sigh, Mr Kinnear exchanged his giant boring clumpers for Tom's weird raised trainers. Poor Mr Fuller's look of pure relief when Tom turned up again, in full school uniform, was worth the trouble of rushing down three corridors and arriving hot and panting. He ordered the hooting to stop at once, hushed up the wolf-whistlers and the gigglers, rushed Tom to his place, and even managed to start the exam on time. I reckon he'd have brought a tea tray to Tom's desk if it had been allowed, such was his gratitude at being saved from letting a moment's irritation blight a young man's start in life (and the blistering tongue-lashing he'd have had from Mrs Garabour).

Stol was the hero of the hour, of course. (Though Madge did earn a certain sort of dark respect for walking round for two whole hours in Tom Dunn's grubby clothes.) But all the credit ought to go to Tom. I know worse things happen, even in army training. But Tom will be all right. After all, only a boy of true grit could stride with dignity through a set of double doors, skimpy top clinging to his chest, a girl's skirt flapping at his hairy thighs, and, enduring the gauntlet of two hundred watchful pairs of eyes, sit down, and then pass, quite a stiff examination.

The moment Mum went off to buy her billionth cup of coffee, up oiled this woman. I think I have the gift of spotting people out of uniform. I was suspicious at once.

'Your brother, is he?'

He might as well be, when it comes to it. I didn't quite dare lie, but did manage to give the impression I'd nodded.

'Bit of a fracas back at the house?'

Police officer, was she?

I played dumb. 'Fracas?'

'Well, from a peek through the windows, things did seem to be in a bit of a mess.'

That didn't sound right. Stol's room might be a pit, but if he so much as leaves a sock draped over a banister anywhere else in the rest of the house, Esme takes a fit. And I've seen that Mrs Leroy of theirs get the floors mopped back up to her employer's high standards even before we're done tracking across them.

'Mess?'

'Stuff all over. Laundry strewn over the floors, and hanging off doorknobs.'

And suddenly I thought: That stupid tea towel with all the knots! If I'm honest, I was furious. If he had been awake, I honestly believe I might have socked him on the first bit I could find that wasn't broken. How could your best friend even *think* of—? How could he even *imagine*—?

But this police officer in disguise was watching closely, and I thought: Tread carefully; don't get Stol in trouble. We have a boy at school who took some pills once. Now they never let him be. Even months after, they still watch Rupert every day as if he's leaning too far out of a window. When he sighs, their eyes narrow. If he makes a joke, they're looking for something behind it. If he dared hand in a poem in the slightest bit gloomy, they'd be making sly phone calls, then listening out for the sirens.

Stol couldn't stand it. No. I know Stol to his boots. He couldn't stand it.

Though I'd not spoken, still the visitor took a seat. And suddenly I wasn't just suspicious, I was positively *sure* that she'd waited till Mum was gone to slip in and ask her questions.

'So would you say that Stuart here was in a state?'

I pretended to give this some thought. 'No.'

'No family quarrel?'

'I don't think so.'

'Things did look a bit – chaotic.'

Well, so they would, with Stolly turning the house upside down to find his tea towel. My mum bought him it. TEN VERY USEFUL KNOTS. It was her last-ditch attempt to get him confident about his shoelaces before the move up to the main school. I was quite envious, as I recall, because it was brilliant. It had instructions for the Flemish Loop,

102

the Carrick Bend, the Bowline on a Bight, and seven others.

And which of the diagrams did I suddenly suspect had sent Stol scattering laundry over his mother's perfect floors?

Oh, only the one at the bottom. The Hangman's.

Sickness of Soul

You don't have to be Sherlock Holmes to work it out. Stol's always given much more thought to 'Life' than I have. (Hard to give it less.) He falls into anguish at the smallest things. Only the day before, he'd got in quite a deep spat with Mrs Garabour about not speaking up when we say Grace. 'I *can't*,' he wailed. 'Firstly, I have stopped thinking God exists. And, even if I hadn't, I'd still believe he ought to be doing something a little more useful than hearing me go on about getting a salad.'

So let's not claim Stol never paddles through dark thoughts. But up till now, give or take the odd funny mood on a high car-park parapet, his motto's been 'Onwards and upwards'. Certainly the only time I've ever known him truly sick of soul was when his dad went berserk from hearing Del and the Stompers.

We'd known that Mr Oliver had a tough streak since that business of the devil on Stol's shoulder.

But quite what a dark side he hid beneath those expensive suits and fancy spotted neckties was not quite clear till, for Stol's birthday, I bought Del and the Stompers' *Greatest (and Loudest) Hits*. Stol loved it – played it all the time. Suspiciously, after a week, our music centre stopped working and Dad didn't seem in any hurry to fix it. So we decamped to Stol's, and gradually the din of the best tracks juddering away down the house turned Mr Oliver quite ratty.

First, he insisted we wore our headsets.

'Can't stomp in headsets,' Stol explained to him.

'Try!' snarled Mr Oliver.

But, what with the stomping, of course, both sets soon got broken. Esme came to the rescue, bringing home from The World of Esme a box of two hundred surplus (tr: unsellable) pink angora earmuff headphones. They might have looked good – if you were a child of *three* – but the sound reproduction was rubbish, so we never wore them.

And Mr Oliver got rattier and rattier, till one day, when I was there as well, learning a new stomp from Stol, he cracked and, ignoring me, stormed up and dragged Stol down both flights of stairs and straight out of the back door.

'Get in the car. Now!'

Bemused, Stol stumbled in, and Mr Oliver slammed the door on him, and got in himself. He wouldn't let me come, so I just waved them off, with Stol making How-should-*I*-know-what's-bugging-him? faces through the side window, and Mr Oliver driving in a frenzy over every single speed bump between their house and the corner.

Stol told me after that his dad had driven him straight to the law courts. They'd parked in a space marked RESERVED FOR SENIOR COUNSEL, and people in gold braid had pulled their forelocks as his dad strode past.

'Not pulled their *forelocks*!'

'Well, you know. Scuttled out of his way, bowing and scraping, with many an oily "*Good morning, Mr Oliver*".'

'Showed a bit of respect, you mean?'

'Possibly,' Stol said sourly (though on the whole he was quite proud of having a distinguished father). 'I suppose so.'

'What happened then?'

'He *only* dragged me through a few million panelled rooms with carpets ankle-deep in *fleurs-de-lis*.'

'*Fleurs de* what?'

Stol ignored me. 'Then down stone steps, along a hundred green corridors with livid strip lighting, and through a door labelled VIDEO LINK INTERVIEW ROOM.'

'Weird . . .'

'It *was* a weird room,' Stol confessed. 'Pretend cosy, if you see what I mean.'

'No.'

'Well, there was a warm-coloured mauvy-pink carpet, but it had coffee stains all over it. And though the walls were a nice pink, they had scribbles and scratches so they looked rather nasty. There were even a few pictures. One was of a stag in a forest, but someone had drawn a moustache on it.'

'What was the furniture like?'

'There wasn't much. A couple of chairs in the corner, and one slightly more comfy one in the middle, bolted to the floor.'

'And nothing else?'

'Oh, yes,' he said bitterly. 'A big wide mirror.'

'Two-way?' I asked suspiciously.

'I reckon.' Stol scowled again. 'Anyway, at least by then I knew it was the music that had put him in a bate, because he'd been muttering about it all the way as we drove. But I would never have thought my own dad could have done what he did.'

'What?'

Stol spread his hands. 'Unbelievable! I sat in the only halfway comfy chair and suddenly my own dad's voice is pouring out of these speakers I hadn't even noticed were there. "I'll teach you what it's like, having to listen to music you can't stand! I'll show you!" And out pours this awful, *awful* noise.'

'What noise?'

'Edmund Forlando and his Orchestra's *Song of Strings*.' Stol shuddered. 'It was *horrible*. It just went on for hours. All whiny and swoopy and senti-mental and ghastly. I know it was a two-way mirror because, each time I stuffed my fingers in my ears to blot it out a bit, they turned it louder.'

'Grim!'

106

'I practically came unpicked.' He sighed. 'My own dad! Who would have thought it? Torturing his own flesh and blood with Granny music!'

'Cruel!'

'That's what I thought. And in between ghastly pieces, this awful Edmund Forlando fellow would even introduce things. He kept saying things like, "Now here's a lovely old number many of you will remember. Not only is it tuneful, with a melody to set your feet tapping, but it always reminds me of ocean waves lapping at coral shores. Do even hum along with us if you choose."'

'Oh, Stol! Your own dad!'

'I know. My own dad! Don't think I wasn't in *despair*. But then an odd thing happened. I suddenly realized I'd begun to think about the chair I was sitting in and all the sad souls who had sat in it before me.'

'What sad souls?'

'I don't know. Whoever has to use a video link to give their evidence in court. People who've squealed on drug dealers or Tong gang members, maybe. And weeping kids saying, "Yes, I saw Daddy put the carving knife in Mummy's tummy."' That sort of thing. And there I was, just sitting in it to be played some horrible music.'

Thoughtfully he hummed a snatch from *Song of Strings*.

'And suddenly I thought: Life's so *unfair*.'

And, honestly, I do believe Stol might have cried if Del and the Stompers hadn't been coming right to the best bit, where we have to stamp in unison on the floor and point at the ceiling while swinging our arms round.

Next day, when he was still looking a little bit gloomy in class, Mr Tully asked, 'What's up with Stol?'

I didn't see any reason not to explain. 'He's sick of soul,' I said. 'He thinks that life's unfair.'

'Ha!' Mr Tully clearly wasn't going to give house-room to sickness of soul or life being unfair as excuses for not paying attention. He went over and pushed Stol. 'Think life's unfair, do you?'

Stol nodded mournfully.

'Yes, well,' said Mr Tully. 'Look at it this way. Life's being so unfair is what makes it so *interesting*.'

And he went off to tell Maria to stop feeding Gregory bits of her sandwich.

Stol was quite taken with the idea of Life's unfairness being 'added interest'. Like 'extra bleach'. He brightened up at once. So, next day, when Mrs Hetherington said to him sternly, 'I hope your mind is going to be on what we're doing, Stol. I've been hearing about you in the staffroom,' he answered, beaming, 'No. It's all right. I have decided sickness of soul is a personal weakness, not a valid philosophy.'

Homework

About ten minutes ago, I heard faint tap-tapping on the glass panel of the door at the end of the ward. Since Mum was deep in the problem page of her *Pretty Miss Petticoat*, I got up and went over.

Out in the corridor there was a youngish woman in leather jacket and trousers. She had a motorcycle helmet dangling from her belt and was holding a clipboard. She glanced up and down the almost empty ward. 'Package for Paramour.'

'Me,' I said, adding, pointing to Mum still deep in her *Pretty Miss Petticoat*. 'Or possibly her.'

She looked at the list on her clipboard – 'Ian James' – and pointed to the blanks. 'Print here, please. And sign there.' She filled in the date and time before moving away. I went back to my chair and ripped open the sealed plastic package she'd given me, with Mum sitting there trying to pretend she was still reading *Pretty Miss Petticoat* and not being nosy.

Inside was a thick grey envelope with Stol's father's firm's name printed across the top in curly raised letters.

I turned it over. On the back Jeanine had written, '*No hiding place, Ian!*'

I tore the envelope open. Out fell a dozen faxed and e-mailed absentee homework slips, all filled in by teachers whose classes I had missed today or might miss tomorrow. I was outraged. Quite *outraged*. One day! One poky day! And there they all were, getting in touch through Jeanine as fast as they could, as if they suspected me of spending the missing hours lounging with my feet on the end of Stol's bed, chewing gum, playing hand-held computer games and whistling.

I looked at Mr Bryson's. Physics. '*Describe in as technical terms as you can manage any equipment around Stol's bed. Try and explain the principles on which you think each works. Diagrams will be welcome.*'

Bit weird. But if I'd missed what they were doing in class today, I suppose it made some sort of sense.

Almost.

I looked at Mrs Hetherington's. Chemistry. '*Study the labels on all the drug packets, drip bags, etc., round Stolly's bed. Copy them out neatly, paying* particular *attention to the spelling. Find out what you can about each drug and its uses from the professional staff around you.*'

Maths. Mr Deloy.

Clipped to his slip were three pages of photocopying from our maths revision textbook. His orders were: '*Revise weights and measures, and decimals. Using details from Stuart Oliver's current drug regimen, offer five examples of how a lack of knowledge or accuracy in either could prove disastrous.*'

English was: '*Write about your day. (Three full sides, please.)*'

Clipped to it was French: '*Translate at least twelve lines of the attached into French.*'

Art from Mrs Floo was: '*Sketch what is on all four sides of you. Make each of your renditions as realistic as possible.*'

Teachers. They spend their *whole lives* acting as if no greater fortune could come their way than that the whole class might fall down a cliff and leave them in peace and quiet. And then just one of their charges tumbles out of a window and they can't rest until they know exactly what's going on, how bad it is, and what's likely to happen.

Interesting, eh?

Nothing from Sports, though

Nothing from Sports, though. Maybe that's not surprising, since Stolly wriggled out of games more often than a girl. They use the usual excuses. Stol simply hid.

The habit began one day when he'd just run my blood cold with one of his horrible stories. 'So to get away from the bullies, this kid hid in one of his school changing-room lockers. But when he tried to let himself out again after the final bell rang, he found the catch had dropped, and he was so tightly packed in, he couldn't shift round to unpick it. He banged and banged, but all the pupils and teachers had gone home, and the janitor never happened to come within earshot.'

'So what happened?'

'He suffocated overnight.'

I stared at the five little holes drilled in a neat pattern on my locker door. Up till that moment, it had never occurred to me why they were there.

'But the worst is,' said Stol, 'that no-one realized. I guess if no air can seep in, then no smell can seep out. Everyone who looked at that locker just assumed it was already being used that day, or had jammed shut. It ended up being ignored. Then, years later—'

'Oh, no. Not years!'

He grinned. 'Yes, *years*. The changing rooms were being tarted up at last. Some workman forced the locker open with his chisel to paint the edges, and out tumbled this shrivelled, wizened little body with floating hair and a mummified face. Still in its games shorts and sneakers.'

'God, Stol. That's horrible!'

'Isn't it?'

It didn't put him off his plan, which was to skip games and spend the time scrunched, reading, in a locker. It got to be a habit. I'd keep a look out while he clambered in, and then, when those of us who aren't allergic to fresh air and exercise roared back an hour later, I'd rat-tat our signal on the door to let him know it was us. Out Stol would tumble, grousing about cramp, or numb fingers, and filling me in on whatever he'd been reading in the tiny beams of light stealing in through the air-holes.

'We won!' I'd interrupt. 'Creamed them, five-nil! Jack Warren scored a hat-trick! They were rubbish!'

He'd wait till I was finished, then choose a few more highlights to share from Locker Reading Hour. I doubt if he was even sure which game it was that we'd just played. Stol took no interest in sports at all. To him, they were just boring. If I complained, he'd put me down with some astonishing statistic. 'Did you know, Ian, that people worldwide have wasted a cumulative forty-seven billion hours watching other people chase balls around pitches?'

'No, Stol,' I'd say. 'I didn't know that.' I'd turn away, to talk about the match with someone else. It was the nearest the two of us ever came to quarrelling. I'd charge in there, stuffed with high spirits, tingling and powerful and feeling so *good*, and his sheer lack of interest would really annoy me.

Leroy asked Stol once, when I fell into one of my brief sulks, 'Don't you like any sports at all?'

'Well,' Stol said thoughtfully, 'I've never tried it, of course. But I do wonder if I wouldn't quite like ice-skating, if I had the chance.'

(Our nearest rink is sixty miles away.)

'Or salt-water kayaking.'

(We're ninety miles from the sea here.)

'So,' I said. 'Pretty safe, then?'

113

Oh, yes. Pretty safe. So safe, the Sports staff don't even realize who he is, so don't invent any homework to find out how he's doing.

He might be listening

At a quarter to two, Mum got so bored with magazines, she started pacing. 'I should have thought to bring a book with me.'

'They have a shop.'

'There's nothing I'd want to read in there. You'd think only people who like spy stories and romances get sick.' She swooped on a sheet of paper slipping out from beneath what I was writing. 'What's this?' She inspected the tick pattern. 'Is it a puzzle?'

'It's their depression survey. I marked it for all of us.'

'Which line is mine?'

I pointed. 'And you came out very well.'

I kept my head down while she checked my answers. 'I am *not* irritable. I do *not* have a negative attitude, and I *don't* avoid friends and family.'

'Sorry,' I said. 'That must be Grandpa's column. You're two in front.'

She fell quiet again. But clearly I must have done a reasonable job, because this time she didn't argue with any of the ticks I'd given her. All she said when she'd finished was, 'So which line is Stol's?'

(Not mine, you notice. Stolly's.)

'Do you love Stolly more than me?'

'Of course not. I'd do *anything* for you.'

'Anything?'

'*Anything.*'

I thought for a moment. 'Would you bungee jump into a canyon?'

'No.'

She went back to inspecting my tick marks. Then, after a moment, she raised her head. 'People like Stolly, they're so vulnerable, they make people shiver. Each day they get through is a giant piece of cosmic good luck. You feel, if you ever let up, if you *ever* stop worrying, something dreadful will happen.'

'I don't think Esme thinks that way.'

'No,' Mum said tartly. 'Don't suppose she does.'

I said to her, straight out. 'Would you rather have had a son like Stolly than a son like me?'

'No,' she said. 'Though I have often thought it might have been more sensible if I'd been given both of you.'

'What? And Esme and Franklin had settled for a spaniel?'

'Ssh!' Mum said, waving a hand towards Stol in a He-might-be-listening way. And that's when he started twitching and groaning, and his fingers began scrabbling at the end of the plaster.

We both leaned over him. 'Stolly?' Mum said. 'Stol? Can you hear us? Are you in there, sweetheart?'

'Come in, Number forty-three,' I said. (Family joke since the day Stol sulked for hours in a duck-pond.)

I won't tell you what Stol muttered. If he'd been properly awake, and not trussed up in plaster, he would have had a major ticking off. But all Mum did was say, 'Oh, good boy! Good boy!' as if he were a dog who'd done something clever, and she stroked his head gently miles away from the stitches.

Stol repeated the rude thing. I half expected Mum to change her tone and say, 'Now that's *enough*, Stol,' but she was in tears again, so it was up to me.

'I hope you know,' I said, 'that you are only alive at all because of that jasmine bush. And that was a cutting from our house.'

Mum scolded through her snivelling. 'Ian!'

'Well, it's the truth.'

Stol wasn't listening anyway. 'It *hurts*.'

Mum sent me for the nurse. Her only real concern seemed to be whether he knew which foot she was tickling. When it was obvious he did, she pretty well strolled off again. For all his moaning about how much things hurt, Stol seemed to me to go back to sleep very quickly.

'You're crying again,' I accused Mum.

She lifted eyes that were so huge with tears, I saw my own reflection. 'People like Stolly,' she said. 'It's as if the world's just sitting there waiting to knock the stuffing out of them.'

'And people like me?'

'You're different,' she said. 'You're – what's the word? – phlegmatic.'

'*Phlegmatic?*' (It sounded disgusting.)

She saw my look. 'Oh, I know it sounds awful. But you robust types are the salt of the earth. People like Stol—'

She stopped again. It didn't matter, though, because I knew what she meant. Stol didn't even realize the days of the week came in the same order every time, until I told him.

How robust is that?

Glory everywhere

Which is odd for a person who has so many good times. I'm no damp squib. My spirits rise on frosty mornings, or thudding down hills at top speed. But Stol sees glory everywhere. We'll lie on our backs, sun spangling our eyes, and Stol will say, 'This is *perfection*, Ian. This is the *perfect moment*. I am *perfectly* happy.'

'It's all right, isn't it?' I'll agree, thinking of the sandwiches waiting in my schoolbag. (Nothing as good as Mr Oliver's stuffed olive ciabatta, but good enough for me.) And Stol will prose on:

'No, seriously, Ian. This is the very best moment *of my life*. I am so perfectly happy I could *die*.'

'Wouldn't that spoil it a bit?'

'Ian, you're such a *clod*.' (His way of calling me phlegmatic.) 'But nothing can spoil this moment. Not even you.'

And nothing can spoil my sandwich. So that's all right. Stol is in ecstasy. And I am happy.

Glacier

We sat as Stol slept: me writing this, Mum reading more magazines she'd found in a corner. After a while she looked up from her *Bella*.

'I'm bored stiff. Tell me something.'

Honestly! Sometimes when Dad's not around, you'd think I was simply another spare husband.

'I'll tell you a story Stol told me. There was this couple. They were so in love. Their parents let them marry young—'

'How young?'

'Eighteen.'

'*Too* young.'

'Well, you weren't there, and so they married anyway. And for their honeymoon they went climbing in Switzerland. In the Alps.'

Mum shook her head. Rock faces. Glaciers. To her, it's all trouble.

'They had a perfect week, climbing all day and having dinner by candlelight at the hotel every evening. And on the last day of their honeymoon, the husband slipped and fell in a crevasse. He was obviously dead, but he'd fallen in so deep that they couldn't get the body out.'

'What, not at all?'

'No. He'd slid through this narrow gap and was thoroughly wedged, miles down. It was impossible and everyone knew it, so in the end they held a little service in the snow above, and left the body there, interred in ice, in his moment of greatest happiness.'

'What about his young widow?'

'She went back to England, grieved for a year or two, then pulled herself together and trained as a doctor or architect or something, and led a full life.'

'Did she marry again?'

'I don't know. All Stol said was that she lived to be ninety-four. And when she was sitting at her kitchen table one morning, all wrinkled and feeble, with wispy grey hair floating around her ancient head, a letter came from the Swiss Mountain Authorities to tell that, over the years, the glacier had shifted – hardly at all, but just enough for them to see the body and know that, this time, they could get it out. And they wanted to know if she'd like to be there when they raised it, to bury it.'

Mum stared. 'Did she go?'

'Yes. Up it came, on a roped stretcher. And the body was frozen, of course; and fresh as a daisy.'

'No!'

'Yes! He was still young and beautiful. He was *eighteen*. And she stood over him, hunched, ancient and quivery from age, with rheumy eyes and bent fingers. His shrivelled ninety-four-year-old wife.'

Mum shuddered. For a while she said nothing. Then: 'Stol told you that?'

'Swore it was true. Claimed that he'd read it somewhere.'

'Creepy.'

Her eyes were filled with horror. She stared at him, looking so young and so pale. All he seemed to be missing was the glacier to enfold him.

Whoops, I thought, looking at her face. Wrong story. Definitely wrong story.

Scar

After another *Bella*, Mum told a horror story of her own. 'You know what we talked about earlier? Whether I'd rather have had a son like Stol? Well, when we were going through all those tiresome inspections and interviews to see if we were fit to adopt, one of the things we had to do was tick things off a checklist like that "Depression" one you did for Stolly. Except this was about the sort of child you wouldn't want.'

'Wouldn't want?'

'That's right. Whatever would get on your nerves. Greedy, say. Or untruthful. Selfish. Or noisy. Or sniffing all the time. That sort of thing.'

'Can't see the point. After all, it's not as if they can look at a baby before they give it to you, and know what it's going to be like.'

'It's an *exercise*. And it makes sense. Up until then, people like us have usually only been thinking, Oh, goody! They might give us a baby! This is a sort of reminder that babies grow older, and though you might be able to stop them doing some really annoying things like sniffing without a hanky, you won't be able to train them out of their deep-down temperament, and maybe you won't like that.'

'Sort of, "*Beware! Here be dragons!*"?'

'Exactly. So Geoff and I sat down to do our lists separately, as we'd been told. And since the adoption specialist had left her other papers in her car, to pass the time she filled in one for herself. "My three are all my own," she told us. "But it's helpful to think about things you'd like clients to consider." So me and your dad and Daffodil—'

'Daffodil? This lady was called *Daffodil*?'

Mum ignored me. 'We all sat wondering what to tick. It was interesting. In fact, your dad and I had quite a good long chat about the qualities in a child we would have found a little trying.'

'Absolutely hated, you mean?'

'Well, yes. Absolutely hated. He wanted to tick "sneaky" most. And I was thinking, What if we end up with one of those ghastly children who sits like a lardy lump, taking no interest in anything? I couldn't stand it.'

'Lucky to fetch up with wonderful me.'

She shoved her tiny foot out to press my huge one, 'Oh, not half!' and went on with her story. 'We finished first, and waited while the adoption specialist—'

'Daffodil.'

'– sat there, merrily ticking off her absolute hates, the same way that we had. Then all the blood drained from her face. She went quite *grey*. It was terrible, Ian. Terrible.'

I pinned my ears back. As stories go, not quite as good as one of Stolly's, but getting better.

'She hurled the clipboard on the floor. "Oh, God!" she cried. "I've just ticked off the four things in a child I can't stand most. And it's my Andrew!"'

'Ouch!' I said. 'And no returns within the month for a full refund.' Then, knowing Mum had somehow fallen in the mood for it, I dared to add, 'So, tell me. Any regrets about me?'

I can't think what I was expecting. Certainly not for her to reach across and push the hair up from my forehead. 'That.'

'What?'

'That scar.'

'What scar?'

'For heaven's sake!' Mum dug in her bag for her compact. I wiped the film of powder off the mirror, and then the smear that I'd made doing that, then took a look.

'That? That is *tiny*. You can barely see it.'

'It looked a whole lot bigger when you were small.'

'Still,' I said. 'Biggest regret? This scar is practically *invisible*. I don't even remember getting it.'

'Well, you wouldn't. You had it already when we were given you.'

'P-C-B?'

(Stol-speak for 'before my adoption': 'Pre-Cardboard-Box'.)

'Don't use that expression, please. And, yes. That's what I hate about it. I know where you got every single other scar. But not that one. Yet somewhere out there in the world there is – or was – some other woman who does know. I've cared for you all your life, and I don't. And I hate that.'

She snatched back the powder compact and snapped it shut. She was so wound up I thought it best to drop the whole subject. She picked up a *Sailing Weekly* and flicked through, not even pretending she was reading it, and I went back to my writing. But I couldn't help feeling a little bit pleased, and a little smug really. For, after all, if that's the worst thing my mother has to regret, then she's certainly turned out much luckier than Daffodil.

A tongue so long . . .

And Esme, if you don't like getting notes from school. The problem was that Stolly would say anything. The times I've heard him complaining to Mrs Chambers, 'I honestly can't believe you're teaching us this right,' you'd think he'd be toast. But all she says is, 'Stol, your tongue's so long it ought to have a knot in it,' and carries on teaching.

But that's the thing about him. He treats everyone as if they're the same. It is as if he doesn't even notice some people are older, or stiffer, or more important. I've heard him ask headteachers if they want to swap yoghurts, and excuse himself for being late to lessons by explaining he and the janitor were discussing Mesopotamia.

And no-one puts him down for 'being smart'. Right back since nursery, the whole world's known that Stol has passions, and anyone who drifts in his sight line is risking a lecture on dinosaurs or astronomy, arctic expeditions or insects. His home-made family tree from Genesis spilled over four sides of our dining table for *months*. For my project on Vikings, all I did was take dictation. And since what Stol doesn't know about weather and stuff could be written on a fly's wing, we've always got top marks in Natural Science – except when Mr Pinkerton has made me sit where it's difficult to make sense of Stol's attempts to send semaphore.

The trouble is, he hasn't simply fetched up knowing things. He has opinions. And he speaks his mind. I can't describe how close to tears poor Reverend Hubert got when Stol spent a whole lesson insisting God was just 'the grown-ups' imaginary friend'. Some teachers get ratty. Others forbid him to open his mouth till the lesson is over. Mr Havergill once lost his temper. 'One single word more, Stol, and your head's in that holly bush!'

And most let off steam when it comes to report time. We play an end-of-term game at my house, translating Stol's reports.

'Now this is Mrs Tarraway. She's written: "*Whilst expressing his views with admirable vigour and conviction, Stol could occasionally make allowance for the slightly more tentative opinions of others.*"'

'She means you're an opinionated little cockroach.'

'A menace to her happy classroom.'

'One giant pain.'

Stol doesn't mind. He seems to have accepted years ago that he's not quite normal. I don't think it bothers him. It takes all sorts, as people say. And even when thinking deep thoughts and staring down from high viaducts, he has generally been cheerful. Putting aside the odd bad time, he's always seemed to me to wake to face each day as if it might turn out quite fun. I look at him flat out in front of me, too bashed to wake, and it's hard to believe that his spirits could slip down so fast he'd go after that tea towel, then up to that rafter.

But things in his mind do have a definite habit of turning strange. Take a few weeks ago, when for once he'd been flushed from his locker and out onto the sports field. We took a break behind the roller and Stol said to me, 'Remember that little black devil on my shoulder?'

'Yup.'

'That one I couldn't see because it jumped so fast.'

'Because it wasn't *there*.' I corrected. 'Because you were only *imagining* it. Because you're *bats*.'

'Yes, that one. Well, it's sort of back again. Except that, this time, it isn't a little devil on my shoulder. It's like another me.'

Sometimes he quite defeats me. 'Sorry?'

He put a grass stalk in his mouth and let it dangle. 'What I mean is, I feel I have another self hiding inside me. I know him well because he's with me all the time, everywhere I go. But it's like being haunted.'

'Haunted.'

'Yes. Because he's really my enemy, out to cause trouble, and he keeps trying to tempt me.'

'Tempt you to what?'

'Be more like him instead of me. Do things he wants me to do. Think thoughts he's thinking.' Stol spat out the soggy grass blade. It landed on my shorts, but I didn't say anything. 'And since I really am him too, of course, it's very tempting.'

I thought of Dad, making his curly-wurly cuckoo sign whenever Stol starts up like this. 'So what's he like, this shadow self of yours?'

'Like a dark side. You know, like when they're giving you a ticking off and they say something like, "You know your problem? You're your own worst enemy." Well, he's like that.'

126

'Seriously spooky.'

'Not half.' Stol spread his hands. Under each nail, there was a line of black. 'What can you do?'

'Exorcism!' I shouted, and threw myself on top of him. We rolled about, me shouting all the snatches from old horror films I could remember along the lines of, 'Depart, ye gibbering fiends from hell!' and, 'Begone, foul black devils, I command thee!' Stol played his part, first scrunching up his face in the agonies of demonic possession, then affecting an expression of intense inward struggle followed by pure peaceful bliss.

Then we lay back to rest.

'See that cloud?' Stol said. 'Wheelbarrow.'

'See that one? Double bass.'

The sun came out. That always sends Stol quiet – and me too, since, back in nursery, he first taught me to water my eyes and flicker my lids till it's like being underwater in some delicious sunlit pool. Even the wriggly things that roll down your eyeball can look like idly floating weeds. You're in another world. And even if you blink the shimmering ripples away, you could still be on some delicious beach in Malaga, or pegged out under desert sun, if you weren't on a muddy sports field, half a mile from the gasworks.

The world came back. Up shot a nearby window. Out came Mr Bryson's voice. 'I don't remember hearing any of the games staff authorize a little break for the congenitally idle behind that roller.

On your feet, Stuart Oliver! Back on the run! And take that Man Friday of yours along with you, would you?'

Man Friday

This whole Man Friday thing began a couple of years ago, some time in the summer, when I was put in charge of getting Stolly to exams.

'Not just on time,' Mrs Hetherington ordered me sternly. 'Clutching the right gear. Spectacles. Ruler. Calculator. Wristwatch. Everything he needs.'

I have my dignity. I did put up a fight. And out it poured quite well, since it's the speech that Mum's delivered to me once a week since I was four.

'Stol has to take responsibility for himself. After all, he's got to learn some time. He won't always have his best mate trailing after him, to remind him what day it is and keep him out of trouble.'

Mrs Hetherington said witheringly, 'Ian, you can take all the fancy psychological lines you like, but I, who toil at the rock face of education, simply want him to pass his exams. So you *do* it.'

And no big deal, since for some years now I've been ambling round behind Stol, pointing out books that need taking to lessons, or homework that ought to be finished by Friday. I tap my watch when it's time for his violin lesson. I make sure we drift round the back in time for the swimming bus. The only thing that's an effort is remembering, when I get home, that I have to knock off a bit or I get the lecture from Mum.

'Ian, there are a host of theories about raising balanced children. But in none of them does one boy trailing round picking up after another rate as a fine plan.'

'If you're so good at bringing up kids,' I challenged her once when she was ticking me off for putting Stol's socks in the laundry, 'how come you never had any more?'

'Next door's cat dug up the gooseberry bush.'

'Seriously.'

She stopped sorting the newspapers into piles for the garbage. 'Well, for one thing, we never asked.'

'Why not?'

'If I'm honest, for a while I don't think it occurred to us. We were so thrilled to have you. I suppose we assumed we would think about it later.' After a moment's pause, she added, rather as if it settled matters: 'Then, of course, Stol came along.'

'What's Stol got to do with it?'

She stared as if I'd asked what water had to do with drowning. 'You have to admit he's a bit of a handful.'

I swear she said it as if Stol were ours. Nothing to do with either Esme or Franklin.

'But suppose the Olivers had moved house? Upped sticks and moved away? You'd have been left with just me, and a few fond memories of a neighbourhood nutter.'

'Don't call Stol a nutter, please.'

I wasn't to be deflected. 'Answer the question. You mean, I really didn't get another brother or sister, just because of Stol?'

'See?' she crowed. 'You said "another"! That proves you think the same way we do.'

Off she went, grinning, as if she'd proved her argument. But I didn't let up. Before the two of them could cobble their stories together, I followed the faraway sound of banging from the attic. Scrambling up the ladder to the trap door, I poked my head into the filthy dark space where Dad was lying on his back under the water tank, attacking something rusty.

'Explain to me! Here you are: two parents. There they are: whole orphanages bulging at the seams with sobbing kids longing for Happy Homes. So how come you only have me?'

He starts with the jokes, of course. 'One of you is enough for anyone, Ian.'

'No, no. I'm serious. If I'm supposed to be such a success, how come you didn't adopt again?'

He rolled over and put down his spanner. 'You're a success. Never doubt that.'

'Well, then? Why aren't there more of me?'

He made a face. 'Don't think that no-one's ever suggested it.'

'So?' I persisted. 'Why not?'

He raised a hand against a fierce slant of light

130

splitting the dark from a slate crack. 'Your mum has always said she thinks that you and Stol between you are more than enough.'

'That's what she just told me.'

'She would.' He gave me a long look. 'But, personally, I've always suspected there's a bit more to it than that. I think—'

'What?'

'I think your mum just feels she doesn't want to push her luck.'

'Push her luck?'

He reached out a hand that was covered in rust. Taking me by the chin, he eyeballed me as if I were some hard-faced Alsatian he'd decided to stare down. 'Listen,' he said. 'How often are you going to find a diamond among the dustbins?'

I shook his gritty fingers off. 'I don't know, do I?'

'I wanted more,' he confessed. 'I wanted lots of you. But it was up to Sue. And though your mother claims to be so sensible and clear-headed and all that, I think about this she got really superstitious. I think, whenever we got close to it, she thought, How could we ever be so lucky again? and couldn't bring herself to risk it.'

I've thought about it since. A lot. And what I've thought is, if I were Mum – and I knew Stol – I wouldn't risk it either.

So that's that.

Cobwebs

At half past three, Dad showed up. 'Got off work early.' He took a look at Stol. 'My lord, the boy's made a proper mess of himself this time. Which window did you say?'

'The old nanny's sitting room.'

'Is that the sticky-out bay above the back porch?'

I put him right. 'No. It's the one above Esme and Franklin's bathroom.'

Dad whistled. 'Straight drop, then?'

'Except for the jasmine bush.'

'He'll be grateful for those scratches when he comes to his senses.'

'You know Stol. When he comes round, he's always in a foul mood. He won't be grateful for anything. And he hates being in plaster.'

'Doubt if he'll notice the plaster for a while, what with the pain.' Dad passed me the plastic bag he was carrying. 'Here, take this. Off you go.'

I looked inside. He'd brought a towel, my swim-suit and a couple of chocolate bars.

'Swimming?'

'Do you good. Clear off the cobwebs. To be cooped up all day in a hospital isn't healthy.'

While I was gathering up my piles of writing, he started on Mum. 'And you can push off home.'

'No, no. I'm staying here.'

'Oh no, you're not. You're going home. Just keep

by the phone, and if he needs you, you can be back in no time.'

'But—'

'I mean it, Sue. Go take a *break*.'

Mum lifted her bag off Stol's cabinet. 'You will stay close? You won't just wander off? You will make sure you're here if he wakes up.'

Dad glanced round, clearly on the hunt for something to do. Hastily I snatched up my Stol biography and stuffed it away with the swim things. That left the package from Jeanine. Dad pounced on that. 'What's this, then?'

'Homework slips from school.'

Dad slid them out and read a few of them. '*Describe the equipment round Stol's bed, with diagrams? Study his drug-packet labels?* What sort of homework is that?'

'They're just being nosy,' I told him.

He shook his head in amazement. 'They don't hang about.'

'I reckon they thought them up in the staffroom at break time. And they're so used to sending messages to our house for Stolly, I expect they just guessed that the grapevine works both ways.'

Dad was still shuffling through the bits of paper I'd been sent. '*Make sketches of what's on all four sides?* Have you done it?'

'No. Not yet,' I admitted.

He stuffed the homework slips back in the envelope, and pointed at the magazines Mum had left lying about. 'Have these got problem pages? If they have, I'll be all right for a while.'

He ushered her towards the doors. 'Go. Go. Drop Ian at the pool. And, if you have to start weeping, then for heaven's sake stop driving.'

All-encompassing dark moments

I took the fast lane. Most of the time I swim in the unroped area, even if I'm alone. But this time I felt like grinding out the lengths. Swimming for swimming's sake. The counting started, the way it always picks up in your brain. First the mind-numbing little calculations: if I'm doing sixty lengths, then when I pull level with that set of steps, I'll have done two-sevenths. Then, as you settle, the more fanciful thinking: if Stol's in plaster for – say – eight weeks, and one of those is half term, he'll miss seven school sessions and eight Sunday morning swims. So that'll be fifteen whole hours of his life not spent in water.

And suddenly I was thinking about myself. If I'd swum once a week since I was four, then even allowing for sickness and holidays, I must have come here getting on for five hundred times, which is three weeks in water I'd have missed if I'd never been born – or not been found, which Mum claims is impossible, since, contrary to what Stol claims, I wasn't stuffed *inside* the cardboard carton, but laid in it very comfortably, with all the flaps open. Mum says it's obvious that I'd been arranged that way precisely so I'd be seen and rescued. (It was dustbin day morning.) And, far from being some poor, neglected reject, I'd clearly just been fed a nice warm bottle of milk (I definitely wasn't hungry), was chubby as a bun, and the blanket I was wrapped in had been pinned to my jacket so, however much I wriggled, I couldn't fall out of it.

'So, if she cared so much . . . ?'

'Ian, we'll never know.'

We have our theories, though. We have decided that she couldn't have been a schoolgirl because I was at least three weeks old and she couldn't have hidden me that long. She couldn't have been stupid with alcohol or high on drugs because the whole thing was too organized, and I was too clean. She can't even have made some daft decision she regretted straight away, because my photo was splashed all over the papers for ages afterwards with headlines like: COME BACK. YOUR DARLING BABY NEEDS YOU! and whole paragraphs making it clear that they don't send new mothers to jail for losing their nerve for a day or so. They help them.

No. Can't have been that.

Mum thinks she's dead. She thinks she watched till I was found—

'*Watched?*'

'I'm sure she did, Ian. After all, wouldn't you?'

– and then went off in some strange, awful, dark mood. And by the time my bonny, beautiful face got in the papers to bring her back to her senses, she'd probably already drowned or hanged herself in one of those strange, all-encompassing dark moments some people get when they can't see things in the round.

People like Stol.

I've chummed him through some bad times, I can tell you. I'm not prepared to write about them here. They're far too private. All I will say is that I've come to recognize a sort of mood that Stolly falls in, a kind of cosmic exasperation, and when it happens I take very good care to make sure we move off the viaduct, or play away from the train line. I don't know how his mind works. (Not like mine.) All I know is that Stol never seems to have quite so much pinning him to earth as I have.

And he is half in love with death.

We've always quite enjoyed a funeral. Ever since we were small, Mrs Potter has let us in her shrubbery, to watch them. When we grew older, we worked a serviceable hole into her back hedge to wriggle through into the cemetery and climb one of the yews to see better. Now that we're pretty well grown, we're a good deal more sensible. We check out the times, and go over the railings.

Stol looks up from the paper. 'Hey, Ian! Dig'n'drop at two o'clock.'

'Don't call them that,' Mum scolds. 'It's deeply disrespectful.'

'That's what they do.'

'Oh, no, it isn't. They don't "drop" anything. They gently lower. On ropes.'

Who does she think needs telling? Stol and I have watched a bunch. I quite enjoy the mechanics of the thing. The way the coffin sways, and how everyone shifts their weight hastily whenever anyone stumbles. The way they anchor the ropes so the coffin never splats down. How they have pegged tarpaulins over the dug-out mound to hide the fact it's a pile of dank earth that'll weigh on that body for ever and ever.

Stol takes more interest in the social side. Who's elbowed to the front. Who's legged it to the most important car. He points out the ones who are peeking at their watches, resentful of even the time spent burying a relation who they're probably still hoping has left them some money.

His speciality is eye-dabbers. 'She's real,' he'll tell me, pointing. 'But black feather hat over there is faking. So is that thin bloke on the end.'

'How can you *tell*?'

'I don't know. I just can. I'll tell you who's really upset here.' He'll nod at some drab figure I've not even noticed, but, now that Stolly points it out, looks on the verge of heartbreak.

After, he'll plan his own memorial service. 'Hymn practice first.'

'We all know all the hymns.'

'Not Uncle Lionel. And Maeve and Tilly are the sort who open their mouths but are only pretending.' He'll be speaking in such a forlorn tone, you'd think the occasion had been arranged for tomorrow. 'And Aunty Dolly only sings the notes that aren't too high or low.'

'Better than being one of those ghastly ladies who cranks up to warble over everyone, even though no-one else is even managing the main tune.'

He shook his head. 'It'll be dismal. I know it will.'

'You can't *make* people come to a hymn practice first.'

'I can. I'll write it in my will. "*Doors locked at 2 p.m. Hymn Practice 2–2.30. Service begins at 2.30. No late admittance.*"' He broke off a bit of yew and started to peel it.

'Don't chew that. It's poisonous.'

'Whoops!' He inspected it. 'Weird to think one day we won't be here, isn't it? Sometimes when we're waiting to cross in front of fast traffic, or we're up on the viaduct, I think: I could decide to die, and in less than twenty seconds I needn't be here. We could just – not exist. Just like we didn't before we were born.'

Good thing we're only ten feet up a tree. I don't have to think up some reason to move us.

He's brooding now. 'No more thoughts. No more feelings.'

'I quite like the ones I have.'

'That's because you're who you are. But suppose you were weedy and ugly and disfigured with acne and everyone you knew made your life misery and each day at school was murder?'

'Well, I'm not. And they don't. And it isn't.'

138

'But what if?'

'I'd grit my teeth and see it as a sort of prison sentence. Or a long test, like getting to be a knight, or a saint. And as soon as I was old enough, I'd clear off to Tasmania and work on some huge farm where no-one came near enough to bother me.'

'Not tempted by oblivion?'

'No.'

'No more worries? No more black nights?'

'I don't have black nights, Stol.'

He sees a different world, he really does.

Stolly Rising

★

I Knew at once

When I got back to the hospital, Dad and Mr Oliver were sitting by Stolly's bed, arguing over my home-work.

'Franklin, that isn't right. If you look carefully, you'll see that drip arm is retractable, and I think it's important to show the hinge.'

'I admit I was much more at home with the French.'

'I hope you put in a couple of mistakes, so Ian gets away with it.'

'Mistakes?' Franklin looked up, and, noticing me standing there, asked me directly, 'Do you make *mistakes?*' the same way I'd say to someone from the moon, 'Do you eat *rocks?*'

I picked up some of the sheets they'd finished and pushed aside. 'What about the handwriting?'

Franklin peered at me over his gold-rimmed reading glasses. 'We've worked that out. Jeanine can type it up and say you borrowed the laptop.' He turned back to Dad. 'I'm gathering up now. Are you done with the Physics?'

Dad handed it over. Franklin wasn't satisfied. 'Where are the diagrams? It definitely says on this slip that diagrams will be welcome.'

Dad rooted among the papers on the bed tray, and came up with the diagrams.

I said to Mr Oliver, 'I thought that you'd still be in court.'

He looked up, grinning. 'Case over.'

Game, set and match to him, too, you could tell. I didn't dare make any comment, but Dad spoke up. 'You take note, Ian. Here is the man I want defending me when I murder your mother. His son lies barely conscious in a hospital, and *still* he wins.'

I knew at once Stol must have woken up and spoken. Properly.

I just burst out with it. 'So he's OK? Really? All right in the head and all that?'

'Tickety-boo.'

'If a bit grumpy.'

I nearly did a Mum, and burst into floods. Instead, I asked, 'Was he awake long?'

'Seemed like ages,' Dad said sourly. 'But then again, listening to people grouse about their health is always tiresome.' He levered himself up and reached for his jacket. 'You hold the fort, Ian. Franklin and I are nipping round the corner for a

144

quick celebratory pint before your mother gets back again.'

Franklin looked horrified. 'Oh! I was rather more in the mind for that very pleasant wine bar on Fettler Street.' Off they went, arguing about whether wine in pubs was worse than beer in wine bars. I dropped on Franklin's still warm seat and stared at the pale face on the pillow.

'Oh, Stol,' I said, still thinking of all the good times. 'Oh, Stolly.'

One eye snapped open. 'Are they gone?'

He wasn't in the mood for chat. Mostly, he lay and groaned. At one point he asked rather groggily, 'Is Mum coming?' And though I could have checked with him – 'Your mum? Or mine?' – I thought it more polite to assume he meant Esme.

'Hasn't quite made it back yet.'

Tactful, that 'yet'.

'I feel *awful*. I hurt all *over*.'

'You're lucky you're not dead. If it weren't for that jasmine cutting of my mother's, and me reminding all your nannies to keep it watered—'

'Oh, shut up, Ian!'

He went back to sleep.

I passed the time tidying the bed tray. First I inspected the rough drafts of my homework. (Looked good. They must have done an excellent job between the two of them, pooling their strengths.) Then I brushed off the crumbs from some nice snack Jeanine had no doubt sent along to keep Franklin's strength up.

145

And then, somewhat bored, I went back to my writing.

Esme!

When nurses came along to sort Stol out, I drifted away down the ward. I've seen Stol naked. I've shared beds with Stol. I've burst in on Stol in lavatory cubicles with no locks.

But this was different. I didn't want to be around while they were doing whatever it was nurses have to be doing. And he wouldn't want me there. Either he'd have his eyes closed, in which case my watching would feel like peering through a keyhole. Or he'd be trying to cover his embarrassment by making jokes with the nurses. And since he wasn't on top form, that wasn't fair either.

So I just happened to be up by the desk when the phone rang. The nurse who answered put her hand over the mouthpiece and said to me, 'Someone here wants to talk to your mother. It's a frightful line. I can hardly hear anything.'

Esme!

'It's Nicaragua,' I explained. And then, in what Dad calls one of those moments that give him hope I might one day be an adult, I offered: 'I know her quite well. Would you like me to take it?'

It sounded heartfelt. 'Oh, yes, please.'

146

I took the phone. 'Esme, it's Ian.' The line was so awful, I practically had to shout it. 'Ian!'

Wincing, the nurse leaned back to open the door into the cubicle behind her. I backed in and shut the door. 'Esme?'

'Ian?'

'Yes.'

'I thought this number was the hospital.'

The crackling and whistling were terrible. So was that awful wait while what was said bounced off the satellite. You know it's there. You know what causes it. But still you can't help thinking the other person's suddenly turned dubious and peculiar and suspicious.

'It is. We're in the ward with him.'

'In the *what?*'

'*Ward.*'

'I want to speak to your mother.'

'She's not here.'

'I thought you just said—'

'Listen,' I said to Esme. 'Someone's been with him all day. Right now, it's my turn. Stolly's doing well. He's broken tons of bones, but they'll all mend, and his brain's working fine.' In case she thought my family had far lower standards on this front, I added to cheer her, 'He's been speaking to Franklin.'

'Is Franklin there? If Franklin's there, Ian, put him on.'

I wasn't going to tell her he was off having a pint with my dad. (Or a nice glass of Beaujolais.) 'I'm sorry. He's gone to buy a sandwich.'

147

Another of those pauses that make you think the other person's on the moon. Then Esme said: 'I'm coming home.'

I know what Mum would have done. She'd have slid into top gear. 'No, Esme. Really. Stol's in good hands, I swear. The worst is over. You feel free to stay and finish whatever you're doing.'

But I was suddenly remembering a night when Stol and I sat in our huge pink puffy matching World of Esme beanbags and watched his family's films. Esme flouncing about in a combat-print maternity frock (a seriously weird garment). Then Esme posing beside a font in a church, under a sign that said STRICTLY NO PHOTOGRAPHY! trailing a snow-white lace bundle in a bonnet that I took to be Stol as a baby. 'You were never more beautiful,' Mr Oliver said suddenly. 'Thanks very much,' Stol responded modestly, and Mr Oliver replied tartly, 'I was speaking to your mother.'

Then we saw Esme crossing the lawn in her candy-striped harem bloomers. ('Oh, I remember those!' my mother said later, when I started to describe them. 'They were her gardening dungarees and she looked like Andy Pandy. People would catch sight of her over her garden gate, and then turn and walk past again, silently sniggering.')

The next shots were of Esme peering over the prototype pince-nez spectacles that first made her famous. She overheard my whisper to Stolly, 'Why is she wearing your dad's clothes?' and delivered me quite a lecture about the fact that pinstripe cash-

148

mere flannel went 'right to the core of her aesthetic'. Then we had Esme in steel-mesh shorts. ('*Painfully* successful!') Esme in a chiffon ball gown. ('I know! I know! Whimsy fringing on camp! But a breath of fresh air after all those techno-fabrics.') Esme in a mock shaved-mink boiler suit. ('Don't tell me! You look – and you *shudder*. But, I assure you, Ian, at the time it matched the *Zeitgeist*.') Esme in a plain, severe black veil at Stol's grandfather's funeral. ('Now why on *earth* did I wear that? Oh, I remember. It was because I'd just dyed my hair snow-white for Christmas.')

What I had realized even then was that, for Esme, life was just a show. You wore a different costume for each skit. But that was it. She knew it was a show. And even actors have a life behind.

And Stol had asked, 'Is Mum coming?' His first question. His only question, now I came to think.

So maybe my mum (bound to believe blood's not thicker than water) had been a little bit too quick to tell Stol's mum she wasn't needed.

The pause had lasted a moment too long even for a bounce off a satellite.

'Ian?'

I decided to go for it. 'Stolly was asking for you.'

She sounded definite. 'I'm coming home. Tell him I'm on my way.'

I lost my nerve a bit. Esme is dreadful in hospitals. You really begin to worry they'll pull the plugs on whoever she's visiting, just to be rid of her.

'But what about finishing the shoot?'

149

'For heaven's sake! They're only photographs.'

I felt light-headed. It was the way we wrapped up one of our party games, even when Stol played. The game works in rounds. Somebody says a name, and everyone thinks of something you absolutely know they'd never say. My all-time best was one for Gran: 'I'll just preset the video.' Dad's finest triumph was an invention for Mum: 'How should *I* know where the children are?' (Mum had revenge with 'Oh, no, Sue. Not chips again!')

But when we stop, we have a ritual to wind things up. Someone calls out: 'Esme!' And we all shout, in perfect unison: 'For heaven's sake! They're only *photographs*.'

Tea towels

Next time Stol opened his eyes, I said, 'So what's all this about tea towels all over the floor, then?'

At once he pretended he'd gone back to sleep again.

Next time he cracked

Next time he cracked, I let him have it. 'What on earth were you *doing*? You have as many good times as anyone. More!' I didn't bother to remind him of all the hours we'd spent rolling down Tunney Hill in Mr Baverstock's plastic barrel. Or the times we'd gone fishing with next door's retriever. Or the films. Or the laughs at school.

'Oh, shut up, Ian,' he mumbled.

'Shan't!' I said, irritated. But I did. For what had come to mind was once when we were picking our way barefoot over the stones in the river. Stol had spread out his arms to the sunlight and said to me, 'Hey, Ian, can you feel the ghost of all the other great days we've had down here?'

'No,' I had said, and thought no more about it. But now I did. Now I thought, Do thoughts like that work both ways for Stolly? If he gets low, does he see ghosts of all the other bad times queuing behind the one that he's actually having? Stol is so *different*. Maybe it doesn't really take that much to tip him over. Maybe he's like a water glass under a dripping tap. One last gleaming blob falls, and not just that tiny amount, but the whole raised mound that was sitting on top of the glass then spills over.

He said as much once, when I pulled him off the viaduct. I'd turned to find him sitting on the parapet, leaning over to look down. You could tell he was seconds from – how should I know? Getting giddy and toppling? Deliberately shunting himself off? Seeing if he could fly? I hurled myself at him and grabbed his jacket with both hands to tug him back on top of me. And Stol's no sylph. I hit my head horribly hard on the cobbles, and he scraped his ear till it tore on my buckle.

When we'd stopped pushing one another off, and rubbing bits that hurt, I'd given him the sort of look my mother gives me when I do something stupid, like have a tantrum over some bike chain that won't fit, or some zip that I can't pull.

'So,' I said, in that 'I'm *waiting*' tone of voice. 'What was all that about? What were you *doing*?'

I don't know whether it was the shock of being so close to disaster, or if he was just being Stol. But he made such an honest stab of answering that I was floored.

'Nothing,' he said, screwing his face up and rubbing his ear again. 'Well, not *nothing*, of course. But nothing important. It was just a sort of impulse.'

'To throw yourself off a viaduct? Come off it, Stolly!'

'Well, not quite an impulse. I mean, I was thinking.'

'Oh, yes? *What?*'

Again, he grimaced. 'Hard to explain. But I just suddenly felt "not there".'

'"Not there"?'

'Yes. And not just that weird feeling you're always getting that you're standing outside your-

152

self, watching your own body get on with life without you.'

I could have said, 'Speak for yourself, Stol', but didn't feel it was the time to interrupt.

'It's been coming a lot recently. You must get it too, Ian. Don't you wake in the night with this feeling – this really electric feeling – that something tremendous is about to happen?'

Not wanting to put him off by saying, 'No', I kept my face straight and said nothing.

'You don't know where or when. Or even what. But it feels as if it's getting closer and closer. Everything's sharper. Brighter. More *significant*. You hear someone say something and you think, Yes! Or, when you touch an orange, it isn't just an orange any more. It's—'

I waited.

'Oh, I can't explain! But you feel like a cheat in your body. I mean, outside you look the same, you carry on the same, everyone treats you the same. But inside there's this super-sharp person who really knows exactly what life is and how to live it.'

My patience isn't limitless.

'Not quite so sharp they don't know better than to throw themselves off a two-hundred-foot viaduct.'

'Well, that's just the point, Ian. All of a sudden I just wanted to—'

'*What?*'

'Not be the person on the outside. Not be the usual "be careful" and "you might fall" and "stay away from the edge" Stol. Just for one single moment I

153

wanted to be the one I am inside. The person free of everything, who can just swirl through things as I choose.'

See? Told you. Thinks that he can *fly*.

Well, maybe it isn't exactly the sort of thing they teach at nursing school: 'Find someone really bashed up and suffering, who needs their healing sleep more than practically anyone you can imagine, and then poke them awake so you can have a good go at them.'

But I did it anyway. Prodded him, hard, on a bit that wasn't plastered.

Whimpering, he opened his eyes. I don't think, at that stage, he'd quite grasped it was me making him hurt more. But I poked him again anyhow. 'You listen to me,' I hissed. 'Remember that day when you nearly hurled yourself over the ledge of the viaduct and I very kindly stopped you? Well, that was . . .' – I counted the years back – '. . . nearly three years ago. Nearly three whole years! And you do realize that, if I hadn't grabbed you, you would have been dead all that time?'

He gave me a bleary look. 'So?'

'So,' I said icily. 'Since then, we've had a billion good times. We've had a trillion laughs. And every one of them has been a sort of free gift for you, because, if I hadn't dragged you off that stupid parapet, you would have missed them all.'

I leaned even nearer. 'Would you have wanted to miss them all? *Would* you? Would you rather have been dead through all those "This is the *perfect day*,

Ian"s, and all those "I am *perfectly happy* now"s? Because, if you would, if you want my opinion, it's an attitude of the blackest ingratitude. The blackest!'

Then I shut up very quickly, because the nurses were coming.

The (almost) foolproof plan for suicide

While they were fussing round, I thought about the (almost) foolproof plan for suicide Stol had invented.

'Right. First you hammer a huge strong stake into the ground at the edge of a cliff top.'

I'd looked up from my Maths homework. 'Oh, yes? Why a cliff top?'

'Wait till you hear! Then you tie one end of a really tough rope round your neck in a good hangman's knot—'

'Well, that'll count you out of doing it, won't it?'

'– and the other end to the stake.'

'Why?'

'So you can hang yourself, stupid.'

'I guessed that, idiot. But why *there*?'

'Because you're being *sure*. Next, you drink poison.'

'Poison? What, with a hangman's noose already round your neck?'

'Right. Then you set your clothes on fire.'

'Just to be more sure?'

'Yes. And then—' Stol's eyes shone with the triumph of it all. '*Then*, you lower yourself over the cliff and, as a final touch, just in case, pull a gun from your pocket and shoot yourself in the head.'

'Well, that should probably do it.'

But already he was worrying. 'Oh, I don't know. Suppose the bullet missed and cut the rope in two. Then you might fall into the sea. The water would put out the fire. And if you swallowed enough salt water, you'd throw up the poison. Then some passing fishing boat might pick you up, and, lo and behold, you'd be fit as a fiddle and still on the planet.'

'So,' I'd said. 'Not quite foolproof yet . . .'

'Not quite.'

He'd gone back to his brooding, and I'd gone back to my homework.

A threat and a promise

But at least it had been a plan, not some half-baked stupidity like falling from a window. And it did set me thinking. As soon as the nurses had straightened his covers and vanished, I said to Stol, 'Good thing it was such a crazy thing to do, because it's given me an idea for saving your bacon.'

My accusation of ingratitude had clearly stung. Opening one baleful eye, he mumbled, 'Don't need any help from *you*.'

'Oh, no?' I jeered. 'You've pushed your luck a bit too far to try to make that claim. I hope you realize it's not just my parents and Franklin who'll be on your back this time. There'll be other people too. There's a cop in disguise who is narrowing her eyes rather beadily at your parents. And some woman who goes round scattering pamphlets on "Junior Depression" knee-deep behind her is strolling about clutching a huge fat file on your star hospital appearances.' I leaned closer and hissed in his ear. 'I'm pretty sure she'll want to make a few million appointments, so you can talk to her about your inner thoughts and feelings. And since every inner thought and feeling you've had since I've known you has been very peculiar, I don't offer much for your chances of staying out of a strait-jacket.'

Stol groaned, and, on a winner, I added the worst threat of all.

'Remember Rupert? How, since he took those pills, they've watched him *every minute*? Fancy that?'

Stol rolled his horribly bloodshot eyes. I couldn't tell if what was sapping his will was horror at the thought of all those eyes on him, or plain old pain. But he was beaten.

'Oh, all right,' he told me weakly. 'Save my bacon.'

No need to forget our manners. 'Please . . . ?'

'*Please*,' he whimpered.

I rammed home my side of the bargain. 'All right. I will. But, in return, you have to promise me you'll read what I've been writing.'

He opened one bleary eye. I scooped my exercise book off the swing tray to the side, and held it where he could see it. 'It's your life.'

'My life?' He made the mistake of trying to screw up his face in a look of contempt. The massive fresh grazes across his cheek crumpled, and, wincing, he flattened his features. 'But I haven't done anything.'

'No.'

'Or been anywhere exciting.'

'Neither have I,' I said sourly.

'Or met anyone interesting.'

'Apart from me, of course.'

'Or even had any girlfriends since Tabitha.'

'You didn't even have Tabitha,' I unkindly reminded him, 'since she was imaginary. But I've been writing all day, and I've still only managed to get down the tiniest part of it.'

'Really?'

He took another quick squint at the exercise book I was flipping in front of him. Then at the great pile of sheets on the tray, where the story spilled over.

'All me?'

'Not *all* you,' I admitted. 'There are bits about other people, where you were the one who made all the difference. Or where things wouldn't have worked out in the way that they did, if you hadn't been there.'

Stol lay there, silent. Finally, he said, 'So – a sort of biography?'

'Yes. It's a kind of written Memory Box.'

'Why?'

'*Why?*'

And that, I swear, is the first time I really wondered why I'd spent the day scribbling in such a fury.

I knew the answer straight away though. 'It's to make you see.'

'See what?'

'Exactly how you matter. And how much.'

He made a face. If I'd been anyone else in our whole class, I would have shut up then, really embarrassed. I wouldn't have added another word. But, last year, when we brought home our annual school photos, I'd handed mine to Mum, and Stol and I had stood like wallies while she went pink and sniffy, and scrabbled for tissues. Stol tried to console her. 'I don't think Ian looks that bad.' Mum swatted him away. 'For heaven's sake, Stol! It's not that. I was just wishing so much that I could show it to his mother, so she could know how happy and bright and well and alive her tiny son is now.'

My mum said that, and I felt ten feet high. This book I'm writing is Stol's photograph. Picture of Stol.

So I knew what to answer. Only me.

'I want you to see yourself,' I told him. 'That's all.

From outside. How the rest of us see you. I think, if you read it properly, and think hard about everything in it, then next time you come so close to doing something so stupid, you'll think what it would mean to the rest of us.'

He looked so weak, I thought I might as well put the boot in properly.

'Not to *mention* the fuss you'll cause. Think! This time you're safe, and still your mum's in a dead panic on a plane. You've ruined her shoot. You've probably blighted her poor photographer's career. And you've ruined what may be some poverty-stricken young fashion model's only big chance. Your dad's so distracted, he's probably not prepared for tomorrow's court case. Because of you, some brutish murderer may well get off scot-free. *You'll* be responsible if he kills again, you know. The deaths will be on *your* head. Or, if your dad's defending and does a rotten job because he's been too busy worrying about you, some poor innocent bloke might fetch up in jail for practically the rest of his life, for doing *nothing*.'

I wasn't sure Stol was still listening, but I was so fed up I just kept on.

'And that's just *your* family. You should see mine. My mum's in a terrible state, bursting into tears every five minutes. And my dad says—'

Since Dad had not said anything, I made it up.

'My dad says if there is anything – any bone at all – you haven't broken for yourself, then as soon

160

as you're better, he'll make damn sure he breaks it for you – and properly.'

A nurse strolled past. 'Your friend cheering you up, dear?'

Stol whimpered.

And maybe, I thought, even if I wasn't exactly making the world's greatest effort to lift his spirits, I was doing him some good. I did distinctly get the feeling that if he could have raised himself on his pillows – if only to glare at me properly – then he would have done so.

As it was, he just winced and fell back.

I sat in silence for a while. Then I said: '*So?*'

His face crumpled. Two fat shining tears seeped out. 'I am sorry,' he said in a voice that was even more trembly. 'I'm really sorry. Especially about your mum.' He thought for a bit. 'And the murderer, or innocent man, or whatever.'

I felt a heel then, and confessed. 'Actually, that bit's all right. Your dad was so relieved to see that you'd still got a working brain that he went back and won his case in less than an hour, then hurried back here and did most of my homework.'

A suitably shocked look crossed Stol's face. 'They never gave you *homework*?'

And our quarrel was over. One of the things I've always loved most about Stol is the way he's so *outraged* when I'm treated unfairly.

Cheered, I said: 'You were dead lucky, you know. If it weren't for that jasmine bush—'

He grimaced. 'Don't *feel* lucky.'

Hearing the swish of the swing doors at the end of the ward, I turned to see Dad and Franklin strolling through, practically arm in arm.

'Here they come,' I warned Stol. 'Don't forget we have a deal. I'll save your bacon, but you have to pretend that you're totally dopey. Don't even open your eyes unless they prod you with sharp sticks. And, even then, don't admit anything. Just mutter feebly, "I've already told Ian what happened, and I don't want to talk about it any more." Got that?'

'Right.'

'And do you promise you'll read the book I've written? Properly?'

Either our conversation had exhausted him, or he did an excellent job of sounding fainter already.

'Oh, yes. I promise.'

Saving Stol's bacon

Dad dropped a hand on my shoulder. 'Your mum's on her way up, lad. We just spotted her making for the stairs from the car park.' With a glance towards Franklin, he added slightly uneasily, 'Perhaps there's no need to mention we took a quick break from being here.'

Quick break. They'd been gone forty minutes or

more. But, 'Righty-ho,' I said. Usually I'd leave it at that. But knowing I might want to have him in my power, I gave him a wink, just to make sure he'd grasped that I knew it was a favour.

Franklin looked down at Stol. 'So how's he been?'

Enter the plan! Courtesy Stol's *One Thousand and One Tall Stories*, garnered over years. After all, there's no point being sensible all your life if all you do with the life you've kept safe is to keep being sensible. That would be rather like staying prepared for a giant great party, yet never actually having it.

So, I thought: time to take a risk. Like Stolly, see if I can fly.

'Bit of a rally,' I told them casually. 'Woke up for a good five minutes and told me exactly what happened.'

'Really?'

Franklin slapped on his cross-examiner's expression, and was about to start grilling me when the doors swished again.

In rushed my mother. 'Careful!' she warned Franklin. 'That woman who—'

She got no further before the doors swished a third time and in came the lady who'd been studying Stol's File of Hospital Horrors, followed by the police officer I personally suspected of having swapped her uniform for civvies in the hope of encouraging everyone to incriminate themselves more promptly.

Over they came, while Franklin displayed yet

another of the skills he'd honed in the courtroom. Without even moving his lips in the slightest, he muttered, 'Now everyone leave the talking to me, please.'

'So,' said Our Lady of the Depression Leaflets, when she got closer. 'How is Stuart now?'

I tell you, disobeying Franklin takes some bottle – especially when you have to do it in a bright young voice that pinpoints you for an idiot. But this was no time to toss away the one and only real advantage of my plan.

Surprise.

'Well,' I said. 'It turns out the whole catastrophe was my fault.'

From Franklin, I only got a glower. But from the rest, there was a chorus of blatant disbelief. 'Yours?' 'But you weren't even there!' 'Ian?'

'Yes,' I said, keeping my voice verging on smug. 'It was my fault.'

'How come?' Mum asked sharply, and I could see the policewoman's fingers itch for the pad and pencil in her jacket. 'Would you care to explain that?'

I knew it was going to have to be good, to fool those two. And running rings round one of Britain's cleverest barristers is scarcely a picnic. But you don't hear all Stol's outlandish tales without picking up some hints. So, giving myself time to think, I began cheerfully, 'Well, it seems it all started because of a giant great row I had with Mrs Hetherington in class yesterday morning.'

That bit was thanks to Franklin. I've heard him complaining about it often enough. 'It's always the mix of fact with fiction that confuses a jury.' And that part was true. I'd had a mild run-in with Hethers. 'There she was, standing by her desk, pointing at her boring old Table of Elements, droning on about the properties of something. And I was thinking, if I ever really needed to know it, I could just as well look it up. So instead of listening properly, I was narrowing my eyes at her huge dangly rhinestone earrings to amuse myself making them flash. And she picked a fight.'

'What sort of a fight?' Mum asked.

'She said, "Ian, I don't expect you to smile at me through the lesson with all a television presenter's charm and polish. But there's no need to *glower* as if I've just strangled your cat and hurled its poor body on a bonfire."'

'Seems reasonable,' Mum defended Mrs Hetherington against her own family. But Franklin was getting impatient. 'So how's the whole business your fault?'

'Well, when I explained that I was only trying to make her jewellery wink, Stol started wondering how people tell the difference between diamonds and fakes.'

They were all watching me so intently, none of them noticed Stol open one eye.

'Yes?' prodded Officer Suspicious.

'And that set Stol thinking about real pearls and fake pearls. So he'd gone up and found Esme's pearl necklace. He'd read that if you hold them to the light—'

Not knowing the first thing about pearls, I thought it safer simply to wave an airy hand at this point.

'Well, Stol did try to explain, but he was a bit whoozy so I didn't get that bit. But it does seem that holding them up to sunlight is one way of checking.'

Stol's other eye snapped open. Fearing he was about to rally enough to deliver a short lecture on the testing of pearls, I swept on with my story.

'So, thinking the nanny's room window might be getting sun—'

Now I heard Franklin's brain begin to tick. Quickly I checked it out. The by-pass runs south of Stol's house. The sun sets over the park. So, yes, the old nanny's room faces east and would definitely get the sun in the morning.

Phew!

'So, Stol leaned out—'

'To hold the pearls in *sunlight*?'

'But he couldn't see what this expert was on about. So he was just leaning his elbows on the window ledge, whirling the necklace round and round one of his fingers—'

The policewoman glanced towards Stol, who, with his eyes shut again, looked, and probably was, back in his deep healing sleep. 'He *told* you all this?'

'Yes,' I said. 'You ask the nurse. She'll tell you. He woke up for quite a few minutes. She said I was "cheering him up".'

True!

I picked up the story. 'So he was just sitting there happily whirling the necklace round and round on a finger—'

'That is so *Stolly*,' interrupted Mum. 'He does that all the time with jewellery. Do you remember when he sent my jade bracelet flying halfway up that haystack?'

Collateral evidence! It gave me the confidence to press on with my lying. 'And the pearl necklace suddenly flew off his finger and backwards over in this giant arc, out of sight above him.'

Franklin was horrified. 'What, onto the *roof*?'

(Real pearls, then.)

'Yes. He heard a rattle as they hit the slates and slithered down. He says he thought he might be lucky enough to catch them as they slid over the edge.'

'So that's how he leaned out too far?'

'No.' Remembering what Franklin always said about liars always sounding too glib, I shook my head. 'Stol isn't *stupid*. And anyway, the necklace had stuck in the gutter. So he had a think, and decided the safest way of getting it back was to knot one end of a rope round his body, and the other to the rafter. Then, when he stood on the windowsill and tried to reach up in the gutter above him, he'd still be all right even if he slipped.'

Mum turned pale and sank down on the end of the bed. Dad put his arm around her. Even hard-boiled old Franklin looked a bit bilious.

But the other two stared hard at each of us in turn, still all suspicion. And though, till then, I'd felt a bit uneasy about telling such whoppers, I suddenly realized that everyone else who was standing round the bed knows Stol and loves him. And *cares* about him.

And these two were both simply doing their jobs. (*And* still calling him Stuart.)

So not feeling guilty any longer, I pressed on. 'But you know what he's like about knots. So he needed his tea towel.'

My mother helped then. Turning to the suspicious pair as if she'd single-handedly saved Stol's life, she told them proudly, 'I gave him that.'

Unsolicited corroboration! The best sort, says Franklin.

'He found the tea towel – says he made a bit of a mess looking, but he was in a hurry to get the pearls back before it was time to leave for school. He wasn't sure he'd done his Flemish loop knot properly.'

'It is a hard one.' (Dad was being kind.)

'But he just risked it. He was being very careful, he says. All he was doing was getting balanced on the windowsill when—'

I stopped. Stol's eyes were closed, but I could see the glint of tears beneath his lids. I couldn't carry on. I just felt awful. After all, behind this tower of lies there is some truth he'll have to tell me and we'll have to face. Mum is quite right. Each day Stol stays alive and safe is practically a triumph for everyone around him.

My voice was trembly. 'And then he fell.'

We were all shaken at the thought of it. Everyone was quiet. Then the policewoman spoke up.

'So the pearls are still up on the roof, then?'

My heart thumped. (Always one tiny mistake, jeers Franklin. Always one pesky little detail the criminal forgets . . .)

The only thing to do was brazen it out. 'Well, no. You see, I didn't actually go swimming when I was told to take a break. Instead, I waited till Mum had driven away, then ran over to Stol's house to find them and put them back.'

The moment the words were out of my mouth, I realized I'd blown it. Wrong timing! Stol was supposed to have told me his story while Dad and Franklin were having their drink.

But there was no going back now. Even as Franklin took his breath, I was eyeballing the two of them. 'I think it's very easy, on a day like this,' I told them threateningly, 'to slide off where you're not supposed to be for half an hour or so, without anyone noticing.'

Dad clearly knows when he is on to a good thing. He didn't just keep quiet. He helped. Stepping on Mr Oliver's foot, he told him firmly. 'Well, Franklin, I expect you've been a barrister long enough to recognize the absolute truth when you hear it.'

Franklin didn't quite go so far as to perjure himself in front of a serving police officer. But by dropping his hand on my shoulder he did manage to create the impression he thought I was a fine, upstanding lad, most unlikely to end up in any nearby courtroom dock, telling great porkies to everyone.

She wasn't giving up quite yet. 'How did you get the pearls back, Ian?'

And that's the moment Franklin proved to me, once and for all, that though his salary arrives in truckloads, he still deserves more.

'I'll bet the boy dragged the hose round the front and flooded the gutter!'

She fought back. 'Wouldn't the necklace have shot out the drainpipe and gone through the grating?'

'I expect he put his swimsuit there to act as a sieve.'

She turned her back on Franklin. 'Where are the pearls now?'

I picked it up from there. 'Back where they belong. I used the spare key from the green-house.'

The policewoman folded her arms. 'It's quite a little story, isn't it?'

'That's Stolly for you,' Mum said. 'He must have a file in this hospital ten inches thick. And people worry every time. But all of them have turned out like this – extraordinary accidents.'

170

I put my oar in. 'As I told you earlier.'

The two of them gave up then. I know they'll be back. But, with a bit of luck, Stol will be more on form. If he decides to tell the truth, that is his business. After all, nobody pushed him out of the window. That fact alone will see off one of them. And, frankly, I think the other might learn a lot from listening to Stolly talk about his thoughts and his feelings.

I certainly know I have.

When they were gone, there was the longest silence. I'd had enough of lies. Mum was exhausted. And Franklin and Dad weren't quite sure who knew what.

'I'm off now,' I told everyone. 'I'm actually envying Stol for lying on a bed. I'm going home.'

Franklin rooted in his briefcase for his telephone. 'Can someone sit with Stol for just five minutes, while I try one more time to get through to Esme?'

Whoops!

'Sorry,' I said. 'Forgot to tell you. She's on her way home.'

'Really?' Franklin was obviously thrilled. But it's all right for him. He'll be away in court. And it's all right for me. I'll be in school, taking plaudits for my excellent homework. Mum is the one who'll have to be here, trying to stop Esme drive the nurses so crazy they unplug Stol's machines or overdose him in the hope Esme moves on to make her pesky

171

suggestions in the mortuary. ('Black! So *uncompromising*. Had you considered a more gentle mix? Fawn, maybe? Or light tan? And less bleak coffin linings? I could run you up samples in hound's-tooth or tartan. Or even a nice cheerful tangerine chiffon.')

Content that his wife was no doubt already getting back on form, criticizing the cut of the air stewards' trousers, Franklin lifted a file from his briefcase. 'I suppose, since I'm staying, I may as well seize the opportunity to brush up just a fraction on Crown v. Bellingham.'

We took the hint. Dad put his arm round Mum and, saying goodbye to Franklin, led her to the door. I picked up my Life of Stolly. I wasn't going to leave that lying in Franklin's sight line, risking a writ for libel.

Beside me, I heard scrabbling. When I looked down, I saw that, though Stol's eyes were firmly closed, the end of one of the fingers peeping out from a plaster cast was pointing to his cabinet. Clearly he wasn't feeling tough enough to face a grilling from his fiend of a father on that – or any other – story. But he was offering to keep his promise. Read his Life.

I took it with me, though. It wasn't finished yet. There were one or two pages still to write. And there'll be time enough. Stol will enjoy it more when he is chirpy and can sit up and turn his own pages. By then, of course, he will have told me what did happen. There'll be a new page on his hospital file. And a whole other chapter in my book of his life.

Another Stol story.

Onwards and upwards. But that's how we go.